The Templar Door

An Experiential Journal

Alan Richardson

with

Margaret Haffenden

Alan Richardson has been writing weird, winsome and frequently embarrassing books for longer than many of his readers have been alive and is insanely proud of that fact. He has done biographies of such luminaries as Dion Fortune, Aleister Crowley, Christine Hartley, William G. Gray and his own grandfather George M. Richardson M.M. & Bar. Plus novels and novellas that are all set in his local area, along with scripts of same. He has a deep interest in Earth Mysteries, Mythology, Paganism, Celtic lore, Ancient Egypt, jet fighters, army tanks, Wiltshire tea shops, Great British Actors and Newcastle United Football Club. He does not belong to any group or society and does not take pupils because most of the time he hasn't a clue what is going on

The Templar Door is another totally indulgent book self-published via Create Space on June 24th 2018, the Feast Day of John the Baptist.

I don't have a web site, am not on LinkedIn, and I don't do blogs. A more detailed list of my published work can be found on Amazon Books.

Anyone with a pressing need to contact me can do so via: *alric@blueyonder.co.uk* but please don't attach your manuscripts and ask for 'an honest opinion' because I will always lie.

This is NOT a Templar Cross

Some published books

Geordie's War.
Aleister Crowley and Dion Fortune
The Inner Guide to Egypt *with Billie John*
Priestess - the Life and Magic of Dion Fortune
Magical Gateways
The Magical Kabbalah
The Google Tantra - How I became the first Geordie to raise the Kundalini. *new edition retitled as...*
Sex and Light – how to Google your way to God Hood.
The Old Sod *with Marcus Claridge*
Working with Inner Light *with Jo Clark*
Spirits of the Stones.
Earth God Rising - the Return of the Male Mysteries.
Earth God Risen
Gate of Moon
Dancers to the Gods
Inner Celtia. *with David Annwn*
Letters of Light
Me, mySelf and Dion Fortune
Bad Love Days
Short Circuits

Fiction

The Giftie
On Winsley Hill
The Fat Git – the Story of a Merlin
The Great Witch Mum – *illustrated by Caroline Jarosz*
Dark Light – a neo-Templar Time Storm
The Movie Star
Shimmying Hips
du Lac
The Lightbearer
Twisted Light

Agnus Dei.

Dedications

Greg Hardin of Lo'ville, a truly great man, deeply missed.
Sean Martin for unfurling the Beausant in the first place.
David Walker for two terrific Templar tomes.
Jo Clark for timely and timeless things.
Basil Wilby who tread this ground long before me.

Dan Sandford, Beau Gadsby, Dan Tozer and **Steve Milne** for looking after my wimmen.
Holly Ricioppo for hanging on in there.
Annie Tod who will always be my Lady Tui
Helle Møller our daring Dane from Gomorrah.
Carolyn Moody, earth angel and wise woman.
Joyce Allsopp who was merrily met on Winsley Hill

The staff of the excellent **Trowbridge Library** who were inflicted with my brooding presence when writing much of this.

But most of all to **Margaret** for putting up with me and yet another bunch of soldiers in my head. Now that this project is over she can sit back and relax, and listen to the Silence of the Lambs of God

Contents

The worn, battered, splayed cross itself.

Chapter 1

The Invisible Door

There is a sealed and almost invisible door on the north wall of an ancient and redundant church, in a remote part of the county of Wiltshire, in England. Above the door, and indeed integral to the unusual stone frame, is a large cross *pattée* that sings out the name Templar. When I first saw the cross in 2001 I was completely unaware of that stone frame and it took the awareness of my wife Margaret, many years later, to point it out. Yet there it was, hidden in plain sight. Using this small Mystery as a means of accessing inner worlds, I would argue here that there is also, in each of us, a sealed and almost invisible door that might lead us into ancient and redundant parts of our own souls. The splayed cross which is attached to this one is a powerful inner key in its own right that we can all learn to use.

After my first and almost coincidental visit in 2001, the church in question became lost to me. It was almost as if there was a keep-away spell upon it. I couldn't quite remember where it was, and various brief and guilty trips to the area during my working hours failed to find it. I could get to the tiny church of St Mary, in Alton Barnes, but there were no Templar crosses on any of the walls, no sign of any other church in the vicinity and no-one around to ask. Parts of Wiltshire can be like that: sparsely inhabited but sometimes devoid of habitants. Besides, my life was so bleak in those days that I didn't have the inner spark. I just went into the church and asked St Mary and all her saints to help me out a bit – preferably involving a large sum of money from an unexpected source.

I began to wonder if I had created a false memory. And all this, I would explain, was before the instant discovery available to everyone today via the internet.

I only found it again in 2017 after many benign life changes, in company with Margaret. We parked at St Mary's but then, drawn to the wonderful radiance of the adjoining fields (which some modern pilgrims have described as being a 'portal'), she led me *behind* St Mary's church, across the meadows and stream, through an odd turnstile, crying her eyes out for no reason that she could give. They were tears of what she could best describe as 'spiritual joy' which needed no input or solace from me. I walked on ahead and the past suddenly broke open before me, like a lost door in itself, and there it was, big as a battleship but brilliantly hidden by trees - the church of All Saints, at the neighbouring community of Alton Priors. The name of this tiny village comes from the Benedictine priory and small chapel that were built south of the present church. The Mother house of this priory can be traced back to the Abbey of Saint Georges de Boscherville, near Rouen. Boscherville was a pagan place of worship at the end of the first century AD but abandoned in the third century.

In a sense, the Mystery that I had hoped to explore was being hidden physically by the tiny Saxon gem dedicated to St Mary – though whether the Virgin or the Magdalen I didn't know. Here at the un-signposted church of All Saints in Alton Priors, I saw again the Templar cross - let us call it that – on the north wall. I had a palpable sense of relief at that moment. 'That which was lost has been found,' to paraphrase St Luke. I stood making faint babbling noises but it was Margaret, standing further back, who pointed out the somewhat

Arabic style of the almost-invisible sealed door beneath. Had it not been for her, I would not have seen it.

Documents inside the church mentioned the walled-up doors on the North and South side, noting what they described as a 'surmounting consecration cross' above the former, and briefly mention a scratch sundial with Arabic letters on the tower instead of the usual Roman, and the eccentric position of the chancel with respect to the main body of the church. It might be supposed that the writers had dismissed any mystic Templar connection via that obviously Templar cross. But nor did they mention the two

Clumsily outlined by me. Even so, how could I NOT have seen this door the first time!

sarsens that were *inside* the church, accessed by trapdoors. Or of the tradition that it was built upon an actual stone circle to suppress the original worship. Or of the sacred yew outside, which was 1700 years old. Or the nearby copse wherein sacred waters known as the 'Brade Wyll' bubble up – literally - from the sandy stream bed.

The church itself, dedicated to All Saints, is classed as redundant. This is a technical term which means that services are only held three times a year, and that its upkeep is in the hands of the Churches Conservation Trust. The building is occasionally used for small concerts of sacred music, while the spiritual needs of the locals in the adjoining villages of Alton Barnes, Alton Priors and the hamlet of Honeystreet are now met by the much older Saxon church of Saint Mary, which is bewilderingly close. Why would any society in such a remote area need two churches right next to each other - unless one was for a slightly different type of Christianity?

***

None of this was in my mind during that first visit to the church in 2001. I was in company with two formidable and delightful female magicians: the hereditary witch and herbalist Paddy Slade, and Jo Clark, who had worked with the Sangoma of Southern Africa and later with the Sangreal mysteries originated by William Gray. We were on our way to glimpse the Alton Goddess, so called because the neighbouring ridge of hills, as viewed from the east, show the clear outline of a recumbent, pregnant female with the Adam's Grave long barrow and Milk Hill barrow forming prominent nipples on the breasts of their hills, and Knap Hill the actual swollen belly. More of this Lady later.

But Paddy took us on slight detour and we found ourselves at All Saints. She showed us the massive hollow yew outside that is considerably older than the church itself. People who have taken photos of the tree have spoken of strange anomalies in the prints when they were developed, as they had to be in the days before digital cameras. I posed shamelessly, visualising myself as Cernunnos, but nothing came of my venture. In fact Paddy, seeing me with her inner vision, rolled her eyes and tutted.

Like most rural churches it is unlocked during the day. Anyone can enter and enjoy the peace, although not all churches offer such comfort. I know of one in the other part of the county which has sent some people into raptures and others running out with splitting headaches.

For myself, I felt that that one – or a spirit guardian in it - didn't like me at all. All Saints however was calm when we entered. It is barn-like and lime-washed, with big rustic roof trusses and open timbering. No furniture of any sort except a kind of lectern which is often left on top of the main trap-door. Presumably to discourage or even hide the object of fascination below.

On that occasion the witch Paddy slid aside the lectern to reveal the trapdoor, under which lay a large, holed sarsen that the uncanny Sir Richard Colt Hoare (1758-1838) felt had a solar significance, but which later antiquarians, seeing it supine, deemed to be a 'Druidic Chalice'. Not far from that was another trapdoor at the front right of the church, and a sarsen under there too which she also revealed with a kind of Tra –la! The same sort of stones that would have been used at Stonehenge and countless smaller circles across the countryside. Jo had first visited back in the mid 1970's when she and a friend went there to do some brass rubbings. The church was then in the process of having its flooring upgraded and the whole of the south side had been stripped back to the earth and floorboard support beams. Hence she was in the fortunate position of being able to clearly see the whole of this standing stone, now sadly in two pieces, with the hole in what must once have been the top when it stood proudly erect in its heyday.

It was outside, half-way up on the north wall (always a significant direction for witches and magicians) that I saw the splayed cross for the first time. It wasn't in good shape, but I've no doubt it felt the same about me. After 800 years of weathering that was hardly to be expected. It wasn't carved in the rigid, mathematic exact lines that you might expect from a Master Mason but the unusual inner circles were exquisite, and I can't imagine they would have been easy to create.

'That's a Templar cross pattée!' I told my friends, hoping they would be impressed by my easy grasp of icons and effortless French. They weren't. We went back to the car.

We moved on after that visit to drive around that particular area of Wiltshire, which has been described as 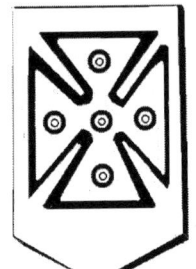 a 'sacred landscape' centred on the massive Avebury stone circle and the adjoining artificial conic pyramid of Silbury Hill. Paddy was intrigued to see a small truck full of soldiers. As ex-Forces herself she went over to ask why they were there. She came back telling us with some shock that a nationwide alert had been declared because of some startling events across the Atlantic. In Britain we would render the date as 11/9/01. No need to transpose this for American readers. No need to explain that, for me, on that day, finding a Templar cross on a lost church suddenly seemed a very small incident indeed.

***

When All Saints was first built, in the 12th Century, it would have been relatively easy to find, though not without physical effort: Head south along the ancient trading route over the hills known as the Great Ridgeway, keeping the vast stone circles of Avebury to the distant right, come down from the heights at West Kennet, continue south and find the copse of the 'BradeWyll'. From there, face east, and after an arrow's flight through more trees, you will come to a large field and the almost hidden All Saints Church.

Today you can find it via the grid reference on the Ordnance Survey Map: Sheet 173, SU108621.

Or if you live in another part of the world entirely you can descend from space via Google Earth by setting the co-ordinates to 51° 21' 28.88" North, and 1° 50' 45.03" West.

Yet in truth these figures will get you nowhere. What that Templar cross above the near-invisible door has made me realise is that we all have an area within our psyches that can be opened. The cross itself, while having an historical style from an historical era, is in itself timeless. It is equi-armed, and links with Elements, Sacred Directions, and all manner of Correspondences and magickal archetypes. It is as much a mandala as the Yin-Yang and as capable of infinite study. The actual image becomes like the icon on the desktop of a modern pc. Touch it, or click on it, and a window will open. Your mind will become informed. Your consciousness will expand – not immediately, but inevitably.

***

Frustratingly for me writing this, it has become a cliché among self-styled celebrities (whatever they are) to describe their own careers as 'Journeys' – always with a capital J. At the same time there is a tidal wave of books today that regard the Templars as exemplars of arcane and dangerous knowledge that is still being preserved by a spiritual elite. Some of whom are, one supposes, disseminating knowledge piecemeal as they hint at their own awesome Journeys. So I have a certain reticence in putting both terms together and describing the present book as some kind of 'Templar Journey'. Yet, embarrassingly, that is exactly what it is, though I will shoot any editor who tries to use that as a blurb.

Or if you want to look at this book from another angle then you might want to think of it as a treatise which might be entitled, not in any way tongue-in-cheek: *Make Your Own Templar Adept.*

In due course I will write about how and why the Templars were formed, how they developed, and sketch as much about their beliefs as any modern commentator can, before outlining their demise and discuss some of the extraordinary legends that have developed since. This will not pretend to be a scholarly work.

What I hope to achieve is summed up in the famous symbol which is supposed to represent their beginning in poverty, when they had to use one horse between the pair of them. I want my reader – male or female - to be the second knight, carried along by yarns, reaching toward the black and white battle flag known as the Beausant that they will one day wave for themselves.

Although I've never been on an actual horse in my life, I am actually surrounded by them here in Wiltshire where massive icons are carved into the chalk of the hillsides. In fact if you stand with your back to

the Templar door you can look across to the White Horse of Alton Barnes and use that as something of a template. Although this one wasn't created until 1812 it has its own energy. Recently, it was illuminated by candles every winter solstice for over ten years, as well as honoured with a lantern parade to celebrate the horse's 200th birthday. It has also been transformed into a zebra on April Fool's Day on two occasions.

In fact there is a lot of personal magick[1] that you can do with the image of a white horse. With this, and that splayed cross above the sealed entrance, I plan to make several actual field trips with my wife to Templar sites across 'our' area. I will write up what we experience – if anything – on all levels. And do my best to help you all crack open your own inner doors to see what lies behind. You won't have to move any further from your own couch or pay for: on-line tuition, texts for further reading, membership of, and initiation into, my gang. And if you experience any kind of journey of your own please write and tell me but do use the lower case 'j'.

***

I had no interest in Templars until, in Paddy's home at North Stoke, one of her visitors that day looked me up and down. Ray, an aeronautical engineer, had been telling me about his experiences at the stone circle of Arbor Low, in the White Peak area of the Peak District. After a pause in the conversation in which Paddy's monstrous dog rampaged around the sitting room, he said:

'There's an old Templar standing next to you.'
'What does he want?'

'He's just standing, holding the hilt of his sword, with its point in the ground. There's a resigned air about him. He's clearly waiting.'

'Waiting for what?'

The man shrugged and went on to tell me about the 'release work' he had done for Australian soldiers killed on the battlefields of the Somme in the Great War.

Now that interested me far more than any Templar revenant, and inspired by what Ray had said I tried to do similar work, many years later, for a cluster of earthbound souls at Hill 60 where my grandfather had fought.

I am not sure when 'Templardom', if I can call it that, re-appeared in my life. But there was certainly a crucial moment when I was in the grounds of St Mary the Virgin, at Limpley Stoke. This ancient church had become by this time one of my own personal 'holy places' for lots of reasons and non-reasons. Arthur and Jenny Firth, the parents of the woman who used the pen-name 'Dion Fortune' had been married here a century before, and I had not long finished the first biography of that extraordinary magician. The church itself acknowledged that it had been built upon a pagan holy place, which had been where the western wall curves above the Valley of the Nightingale. Here, within that curve, her grandparents were buried. And in the ground were – are – 13 Anglo-Norman graves, some of them with swords and faces and bodies carved on the slabs.

I will confess two things here, both of which I will come back to: When I wrote my book *Spirits of the Stones* I had a tendency to see any hump in the ground as a lost barrow, radiating energies; any old rock as the remains of a forgotten stone circle. Likewise in Limpley Stoke there is absolutely no proof that these tombs, officially recognised as 'Anglo-Norman', had anything to do with

Templars. My desire to find occult marvels in this most marvellous of sites may well be creating modern myths - although I will add in my defence that numerous psychics whose abilities I respect have agreed with me about this.

One day, on the anniversary of Arthur and Jenny Firth's Wedding, I was walking past one of the graves when I spontaneously made the sign of the cross and said *Pax Vobiscum*. At which I heard, clairaudiently, the return words from the grave *Et Tibi Pax*.

This astonished me. I am not clairaudient. I have only ever had one such communication before this in my life and that 'message' was absolute nonsense. I did not know Latin. I had no idea what had been said to me, and this was in the decades before the internet made everything instantly accessible. Eventually I learned that it meant *Peace to You* although I still don't know if this is good Latin or not.

I went back many times and said *Pax Vobiscum* to the same grave – to all of them – but I never got another response. Perhaps my first utterance had sent a lonely soul on his way?

***

As to that confession…

I have since learned from mystics and magicians and everyday workers with Earth energies that places can indeed be imbued with power. The man who noticed the Templar standing next to me had recently been 'charging' some of the concrete inserts in the vast circle at Avebury, with the help of inner sources. Did I believe him? Yes, because even if other sensitives felt that the concrete lumps were still no more than that, to the man himself they had become charged with both energy and meaning, and the circle as a whole was now unbroken. He made it work for *himself.*

I have known ordinary household items become charged with power over time. Simple sticks and bowls can become wands and chalices. Gardeners can transform their plots into places that are alive on more than one level, as anyone who has been to Findhorn can testify. It charmed me some years ago to see the advice given for creating a frog pond: 'Build it and they will come,' someone wrote, rather tongue-in-cheek, echoing the tag line of the film *Field of Dreams.* I couldn't see how this would work in in our small garden as we were not near any sources of water or likelihood of frogs from neighbours. Yet…we built it, and they came.

It is the same with inner beings. The moment you think of them, they become aware of you. Deliberately invite them into your home or garden, offering respect and asking for mutual sharing and they will come. You might not 'see' them in any visionary way but they will be present, and like any invited guests will have the potential to cause turmoil

Which brings me to the question of 'Holy Places'. I get somewhat tetchy when people bang on about Glastonbury, in particular, as the 'holyest earthe in England' or even the Heart Chakra of the planet. At risk of losing friends and failing to influence people, it is only special to those who want it to be. Like that church I mentioned earlier – the Saxon Church in Bradford on Avon in fact - one person's sanctity is another's vague sense of repulsion. I would insist that everyone has to work and sanctify their own places. You don't need to visit Glastonbury to skim across the waters of Avalon, nor visit Ireland to glimpse Tir n'an Og, or fly to Egypt to unlock the energies of Karnak. This is possible because the whole universe is within you. It is not 'out there'. It is inside you. Your own apartment or house, your garden, your local park, your nearest hill top – in any country – can be turned into Heart Chakras. You don't need to wear robes and burn incense while shouting out mighty invocations, or yet stand naked in woods calling on goddesses.

In a later chapter I will talk about the 'False Doors' that were a feature of tombs in Ancient Egypt and how they were used, and how our Templar Door can become one such. Through simple intent and original effort, hopefully inspired by some of what you might learn in this book, you will find yourself knocking on that sealed, almost invisible door within yourself. In time, it will open.

Although Margaret and I have been propelled under the most unlikely circumstances to find ourselves together living in an area that is rich in ancient sites, there can be just as much going on within the streets of your own town. Many years ago, while walking through a rather dingy, rubbish-strewn back alley in Bristol, I was startled to have the sense of a young and almost forgotten God, of Roman origin. A quick burst of awareness, light and tone. No more than that. Long before that incident, even, before I knew my ajna from my elbow, I felt an upsurge of energy fountain out from the ground at the side of Charing Cross railway station in London. I was pleased when, several years later, Bobbie Gray, the sibylline wife of the adept William Gray, mentioned the very place without any prodding from me. And some time after that, on the shores of a very small, near-frozen lake in Wisconsin, the sense of an indwelling Lake Lady floated toward me like mist.

My purpose in saying all this is to avoid what might be called the geo-mystic flag waving and virtue signalling that goes with certain places and the people who flock to them. I want to show that every reader, no matter where they live, and in what circumstances, can involve themselves in a personal quest matching this one. Yet at the same time not lose touch with the real potentials of the apparently mundane that goes on around.

I am not trying to crack a silly joke when I say the Templars have been done to death. There is nothing new that I can say about their Mystery. I am not chasing the Holy Grail, the severed Head known as Baphomet, the Ark of the Covenant or anything to do with any Sacred Bloodlines. Other writers have covered these topics in greater depth and insight than I can manage here. Instead, necessarily, I will be talking about: crop circles, spirit paths, plasma energies, ley lines, picnics and Close Encounters of the Fifth Kind (including, bizarrely, my encounter with an alien in a shopping centre); past lives, pseudo-Cathars, pseudo-Templar revenants, group souls and Higher Beings (whom I don't trust much) and of course buggery and hum-buggery among the Templars themselves. As I trot along with the reader clinging on behind me I would ask him or her not to call me Al: I don't like being named after one of Aleister Crowley's books.

Simply, I just want to catch hold of the old Templar who once waited patiently next to me in a witch's sitting room and ask: *What does all this mean? What do you want? What is the purpose of this?*

Chapter 2

Listening to echoes

Look back at that Templar seal of the two knights sharing a horse. They are wearing the simplest of helmets that are little better than upturned buckets with narrow slits enabling them to see. This is symbolic of the problems that anyone has today in trying to make sense of those knights and their times: we have a narrow field of vision, and then only when we turn our heads in the directions we think we must. The reader on the back of our putative horse, clinging tightly on to me, will also be hampered by my own direction of travel. On the other hand, it is a splendid, magickal horse and will no doubt take us where we need to go. The Alton Barnes horse faces west and we might have to go in that direction first.

During all this I will be indulging in a series of yarns. 'Yarn' is a lovely word that has been defined as a long adventure story involving incredible happenings. First reference to the term in modern English seems to derive from 1812 when it was a sailors' expression, based on the notion of them telling stories while engaged in sedentary work such a yarn-twisting. But to me it has always been a powerful tool. Deep, pure philosophies that I've read have usually dissolved into nothingness and left me cold. But if they have been vivified by the philosophers' *yarns* then they have often moved me deeply. Imagine, for example, that the notorious Aleister Crowley had all personal history and personality removed from his writings and he was simply known for his intense intellectual analyses of the machineries of the universe. Only a small, hard core of intrigued academics would persist to the end of his works. In this respect I've often thought that in certain realms, scholarship is like the nails in a coffin lid. However, tied in as Crowley's books are with his varied adventures, manifold personal quirks and incredible happenings that surrounded his every deed, millions have been able to resonate. They might not like him, but he never became invisible or forgotten when they closed his books.

I don't expect millions to resonate to my own yarns and quirks: I simply aim to be heard by the reader on the back of this horse we share, who might gain some value from my burbling. Plus, I'll come back to that strange steed of ours later, but in the meantime, I need to outline basic Templar history for those who don't know…

***

Templars were not the same as Crusaders. The term Crusaders refers to that army which was formed to drive the Muslims out of what they saw as the Holy City of Jerusalem. There was nothing noble about that original army of the First Crusade. Apart from a core of religious fanatics who felt justified by God, it comprised hard-core criminals, adventurers, psychopaths, debtors and general malcontents who felt they could do anything they wanted to the native Muslims. And so large numbers of them stole, burned, raped and sold innocents into slavery. These were not the sentiments of Love they Neighbour. Although they should, as Christians, abhor homicide, elements within the church had perfected the concept of *malecide*. That is, killing that which was evil was seen as good. And because Muslims (often called Saracens in that era) were obviously evil, then they were fair game.

Jerusalem had been in these hands for some twenty years and the impulse to make a pilgrimage to the Holy City assumed great importance in the spiritual lives of westerners. Encouraged by the Church of Rome, it became a status thing.

The pilgrim routes across the Holy Land, or Outremer as it was called, were by no means safe. You were as likely to be attacked by former Crusaders as Muslims, but it came to a head sometime in 1119 when 300 unarmed Christians had been slaughtered by Saracens on their way from Jerusalem to the River Jordan at Easter.

It was then that Hugh de Payen and Godfrey de Saint-Omer, along with seven companions, took vows to protect these travellers. The group called themselves the *Pauperes commilitones Christi* – the Poor Fellow-Soldiers of Christ. These original soldiers were genuinely poor and they made a virtue of it. The ruler of Jerusalem at that time, King Baldwin II, was impressed enough to give them to use as their headquarters, part of the al-Aqsa mosque, also known as the Templum Solomonis because it was believed to have been built on the site of Solomon's Temple. Soon after the knights incorporated this into their new name and they became *Pauperes commilitones Christi Templique Solomonici* – the Poor Fellow-Soldiers of Christ and the Temple of Solomon.

In short, the Templars had arrived.

At about this time Fulk V, the powerful count of Anjou, in France, was so impressed by them that on his return home he granted the tiny band an annual revenue. Not to be outdone, other French nobles followed suit. Although the Poor Knights were still not rich, and had not yet adopted the famed white tunic with the red cross, they were certainly on the up...

We can dismount for a while and rest our horse at this point in the time-line. We might also remove our helmets to get some air and widen our visions. The fact is, despite peculiar energies paralysing my computers every time I look for some crucial piece of their history, I am not in awe of the Templars. Later in this book we will look briefly at some of the extraordinary associations that other writers have dealt with exhaustively and far better than I could do here. But even if I met one in the flesh, at the height of the Order's power, I would still not regard him as anything more than just an ordinary man. The reader on the back of my horse is not in any way inferior.

So, at the historical moment described above, in 1119, before they had become enveloped by myths, legends and perhaps a hint of legerdemain, the Templars were at this point just ordinary men who had done no more than go to Jerusalem. In fact you can feel rather sorry for them: The knights could hold no property and receive no private letters. He could not be married or betrothed and cannot have any vow in any other Order. He could not have debt more than he could pay, and no infirmities. By the time of the Second Crusade knights *had* to be descended from knightly stock. This was in an era when people still believed in good breeding and the innate high-born qualities of the aristocracy. To the Templars, noble blood was everything.

Sometimes you have to think: what a waste - and I'll talk about Templars and Women later.

There is a deliciously eerie yarn given by Carl Jung in his *Memory, Dreams and Reflections* which has always thrilled me, and I think is crucial.

In 1916, while wrestling internally with pagan gods that had appeared in his dreams, he became aware of

an ominous atmosphere in his house. He had the strange
feeling that the air was filled with ghostly entities and that
his home was haunted, yet he did not know what it meant
or what 'they' wanted of him.

> Around five o'clock in the afternoon on Sunday
> the front doorbell began ringing frantically...but
> there was no one in sight. I was sitting near the
> doorbell, and not only heard it but saw it moving.
> We all simply stared at one another. The
> atmosphere was thick, believe me! Then I knew
> that something had to happen. The whole house
> was filled as if there were a crowd present,
> crammed full of spirits. They were packed deep
> right up to the door, and the air was so thick it
> was scarcely possible to breathe. As for myself,
> I was all a-quiver with the question: 'For God's
> sake, what in the world is this?' Then they cried
> out in chorus, 'We have come back from
> Jerusalem where we found not what we sought.'[1]

The spirits were Christian Crusaders who realised after
death that no redemption awaited them in the Holy Land.
They felt that they had been deceived by a false religion
and cheated out of their immortality. Jung, via the literary
utterance of his *Septem Sermones ad Mortuos* or *Seven
Sermons to the Dead,* explained to them that they were
mistaken to seek salvation outside of themselves by
journeying to Jerusalem. The real secret can only be found
inside. If they looked inward they would see at a distance
on their inner horizons a single Star in the zenith. He told
the howling spirits that after death the soul goes not
toward the Christian Promised Land but toward God as
the sun or star within. When he told them that, the Dead
went silent and vanished up into the night sky to their

eternal rest. Much later he encapsulated this in a drawing he gave to a friend, the central mandala of which was a Templar cross.

***

I completely accept Jung's tale and the important teaching it holds. I am not sure if Templars will come crowding to my house like that; our doorbell is broken anyway. I had a few more encounters with them in the years prior to my first seeing the hidden door and I'll tell these in due course. Just now, though, I start to wonder if they have floated in and out of my awareness out of sheer disappointment and are simply seeking release. So before we mount up again here is a simple piece of magick that every reader can adopt and which has stood me in good stead over a lifetime:

The first Templars took a series of solemn oaths before their Grand Master that I will mention later without getting dragged down by burdensome details. You, however, must take an oath to yourself, as your own Grand Master or Mistress. You must vow to view everything that happens, every encounter, as a secret dealing between yourself and the innermost spirit of your deities. Don't look for any reward or end result. Viewing your life like this will transform it. Others around you may think you live a spectacularly ordinary existence, but inwardly, everything around you on every level will take on a certain numinosity, as Jung might have said.

Of course, the first thing that happens is that you will make an absolute fool of yourself, because you will still be looking out through the narrow slit of the iron helmet. You won't be able to see the larger picture and so will jump to the most absurd conclusions about the patterns and inner connections that are now becoming apparent. So then you need to learn Discrimination - which is said to be the first virtue on any occult path. But, as William Blake wrote in his *Proverbs of Hell*, a Fool who persists in his folly becomes wise. He also wrote: 'Thus men forgot that All deities reside in the human breast.' Take this oath to yourself and you will begin. As you do so, be aware that you have now become an Initiate, for that is all the word actually means. Thus we are all Beginners. If any self-styled adept claims to be more than a Beginner then you should make your excuses and leave, while holding firmly onto your wallet and watching your back.

If they get snotty then point out that the dreadful C.W. Leadbeater who took the Theosophical Society into a dead-end from which it has not yet emerged was by his own assessment a Great Initiate. So was Heinrich Himmler.

And a final word of advice before we trot along: Never inflict your personal revelations on anyone else because they won't be impressed and will write you off as being somewhere between a nutter and a crashing bore. I speak from personal experience. Learn the other virtue of Silence, but hold your increasing revelations close, like armour, and please don't become pompous and weird. The last thing I want on the horse behind me is someone yelling that they're being transmogrified.

Now let us have some more basic Templar history so we know what we're up against and can meet them head on....

***

King Baldwin sent Hugh de Payen back to France to raise recruits. The king also wrote to the formidable abbot of Clairvaux, Bernard, suggesting that this new group would be worthy of his support. Saint Bernard, as he became twenty years after his death, was one of the movers and shakers of the 12th Century world. After the death of his mother in 1112 he was sent to found a new abbey at place known locally as Wormwood. He changed the valley's name to that of *Claire Vallée*, which meant Valley of Light, which later evolved into *Clairvaux*.

He was combative, opinionated, devious and ruthless. Toward the end of his life he was called upon to combat heresy in southern France in 1145. That is, he went among the Cathars and tried to bring them back into the fold of the True Faith. To be fair to the man, his final assessment was that while their doctrines were clearly in error, their behaviour and mode of living was irreproachable.

I'll come back to the Cathars later, and yarn about their own nudges on my life today, but we need a quick look at this concept of heresy before moving on, because the very name 'Templar' became a watchword for all manner of great and almost unspeakable sacrileges. If I bristle with rage and upset the horse, then just hang on…

***

In the safe realms of the 20th and 21st Century anyone with an alternative attitude toward religion tends to think that the heretics tortured and burnt at the stake in the medieval era were largely witches, or proto-witches, found guilty of belonging to covens, remnants of a secretive and ancient Fertility Worship. That did happen, and disgracefully so, but the most damned and disgusting heretics of all, in the eyes of the infallible Popes, were two Englishmen named John Wycliffe and William Tyndale. Their sin? They translated the Bible into English, thus putting the teachings of Jesus within reach of the common folk, challenging the absolute infallibility of the Roman Church and planting the first seeds of the Reformation and ultimately the Enlightenment.

In the eyes of Rome anything that defied the power of the Pope and his priests reeked of sulphur. I have no interest in the Templar deeds and misdeeds in all those Crusades which sought to free the Holy Land of infidels. We are still feeling the after-shocks of those wars today, a thousand years later. Simply, the sites of Outremer are not holy to me, today, even if I do seem to have had a couple of unexceptional and sad past lives among the Benedictines. I do feel a certain thrill to learn that the Templars refused to join in the Albigensian Crusade that sought to destroy the Cathar 'heretics' in the Languedoc, in what we now think of as southern France.

Yet there does seem to have been an inner core of Templars who had an agenda and spiritual direction quite different to that of Rome: a direction which might have horrified the rank and file of the Order. We'll try to peek at this inner core soon, as I learn more about this Hidden Door, but my attitude is that from the Council of Nicea in 325 onward, the Roman Catholic Church has been one of the most evil organisations of all time.

Which is one of the reasons I have, at this moment, a certain leeriness about those Templars who seem to have been nudging me during the writing of this. I don't think they were high-grade figures within the Order, but probably more akin to what Lenin might have called 'useful idiots'.

If there are any revenants behind that Templar Door I *do* want them to be heretics in the eyes of the Popes. I *do* want them to be guilty of whatever necromancies Pope Innocent III accused them of in 1208. When I look back at the exoteric details of the historical Order I see the nearest equivalent today in the hedge fund managers, the merchant bankers and stock market manipulators who style themselves as Masters of the Universe. And I want – need – to believe that in the very heart of the Templar egregore, they were better than that, and had the purity of both Light and Darkness that you can find in the Yin Yang – and also the battle flag of the Beausant.

Still there behind me?

***

Back in France, the famously austere abbot Bernard was impressed by Hugh. This was not one of the 'singing, wailing' monks that had so often been sent to the Holy Land to sort out its problems: this was a warrior, fighting for Christ. In 1129, at Troyes, before a convocation of church leaders lead by Bernard himself, Hugh presented the assembly with a Rule. It was a simple enough thing: attendance at services together with the canons; communal meals; plain clothing; simple appearance and no contact with women. If they were away fighting, or guarding pilgrims, they could replace attendance with the recitation of the paternoster. They were also allowed a horse and a small number of servants. They owed their obedience to the Grand Master. The assembly, perhaps over-awed by the fanatical Bernard, gave their approval, but it did command them to drop certain unorthodox practices. What these were, no-one knows.

Bernard then fine-tuned their home-made Rule with his own Latin Rule which enjoined the Templars to renounce their wills, hold worldly matters cheap, not be afraid to fight and always be prepared for death and the bliss of Salvation which would follow. They were to wear white, the hair on their heads to be cut short but their beards left unshorn. Foul language and displays of anger were forbidden, as was any kind of dirty talk about past misdeeds.

Using the full authority of the Church, Bernard thus created a new type of Order that combined knighthood with religion, and by 1139 Pope Innocent II established the Templars as an independent Order within the Catholic Church, answerable to no-one but the Pope himself.

Despite the austerity of the Rule young men from noble families across Europe flocked to join, although it seems that many did so on the basis of a few years rather than a lifetime. There was no money in it, supposedly, but the prestige was divine. Their parents would have approved: their young milord was at last subject to discipline, kept away from troublesome women, was able to have the adventuring that young men crave and would then return home ready to appreciate the world and their responsibilities. In short, they were no different to the young people of today who join up and serve their country in some – hopefully exciting - way.

But what really transformed the very first group of Templars into something rather bewildering and indeed odd, was the fact that at some short time after they moved into their first headquarters in Jerusalem they started digging. It was this single act that propelled them into the realm of myth and legend from which they have never emerged.

The problem with any myth is that it can be pernicious. Like the modern scourge of Japanese knotweed once it takes root it can grow at enormous speed and actually cause damage to existing structures by targeting weak points, such as cracks in apparently solid belief. Before long it can bring about actual collapse.

When those first nine knights adopted the area known as King Solomon's Stables as their headquarters, they would already have been aware of the rumours that treasure had been hidden beneath there after the fall of the Second Temple of Jerusalem in AD 70. Although countless secular buildings across the West have accumulated tales of hidden tunnels accessed via secret doors, there is no doubt that the Templar tunnels existed. As late as 1968 a team of Israeli archaeologists re-discovered these and saw that they led straight under the Dome of the Rock which is so sacred to Muslims today. However, protestors forced them to seal it off again.

The crucial questions remain: What were they looking for? Did they find anything?

This is when Myth becomes knotweed. You can cut off stem, crown and rhizome of the speculations but still it will grow. You can flail at it with reason, logic, scholarship and dogma but it simply spreads the nodes further, taking root before you know it.

I speak from personal experience here too.

The clearest commentator on all this is Sean Martin who sums up their notional discoveries as:

> Speculation has been rife… that they found one or more precious relics from the embalmed head of John the Baptist to documents pertaining to the true origins of Christianity – proof that Jesus survived the Crucifixion, was married and had a family with Mary Magdalen, or that the real

Messiah was John the Baptist - and/or the Ark of the Covenant. Then again, maybe they had unearthed the treasure of the Second Temple which was known to have been comprised of gold and other precious metals and stones. [2]

Not to mention the Holy Grail, the Holy Shroud, the Philosophers Stone, the Emerald Tablet of Hermes Trismegistus or a lost gospel handwritten by Jesus which showed that God was within them. Anything and everything could have been found within those tunnels. (And if the reader on the back of our horse wants more then they need simply invoke the legendary Library Angel and all sorts of treasures will fly toward them. Although, if my rider is young, then they are as likely to invoke the Google Angel in this day and age.)

It just seems odd that the great and good of the Christian world suddenly fell over backward to give large amounts of money and support to a mere nine knights who offered to protect all the pilgrims from the Saracen hordes. Numbers would have been against these knights unless they had superhuman powers, which they did not. No sponsor or donor with any brain would have found their offer credible. There are times when I have wondered if the sudden wealth of the Templars arose from nothing more mystical than creating the world's first Ponzi scheme. This, along with pyramid schemes, is based on fake investment when a group of people (the Templars, say) promise people payment, services or ideals, mainly for enrolling other people into the scheme or training them to take part. The scheme never supplies any real investment or sale of products or services to those lower down the ladder.

Remember that the Order became known as much for its handling of other peoples' money as for its military prowess. They rapidly became the first international bankers, devising a system of credit notes whereby money deposited in one preceptory could be withdrawn at another on production of an individually coded credit note. They kept meticulous financial records of all their transactions, large or small and sent out regular statements to regular clients. In short, they understood money, and knew how to follow it. So if it was simply that, a Ponzi scheme created in an era when no contemporaries had the savvy or experience to see through it, then no wonder the Templars fell out of favour in the fullness of time.

However, standing before that splayed cross on the north wall of All Saints Church, I don't think it was that. 'Follow the money' is a popular phrase in business and government which suggests a money trail or corruption scheme within high office. But here in the middle of Wiltshire I would rather 'follow the myth' and look for riches of a different kind. Standing on tippy-toe to touch the bottom arm I think of St Bernard saying: *What is God? Length, breadth, height, and depth.* This carven cross has all of these. I hope to show later how we can make simple rituals out of its four-fold nature but for the moment I have to look at an aspect of the Knights Templar that is less than attractive to me: it's uber-masculine nature. The last thing I want is to ride the horse of my psyche through hordes of woman-shunning males.

Chapter 3

Templars and their Women

I wrote earlier that anguished Templar shades were not likely to come into my house as they came into Carl Jung's. I am not so sure now. Over the past few days there has been a prickly air in every room and Margaret and I have been somewhat tetchy. Did our moods create this atmosphere? Or did fragments of Templar souls, annoyed with my apparent lack of respect, affect us? I am not psychic enough to get that level of communication. Later, I will go around each room with a small brass bell that belonged to Margaret's parents, which has a curious tone that shivers the air, and ring us back to peace. This bell is, I suppose, an example of a simple household object which has developed its own *mana* over the years.

Meanwhile…

***

There is something odd about Saint Bernard. Much of his Latin Rule was as you might expect: two communal and silent meals a day at noon and dusk. Meat only three times a week. No-one to get down from table except to attend to the all-important horses. Matins at 4.00 am followed by a brief nap; Prime at 6.00am when first mass of the day was said. Terce at 8.00am and Sext at 11.30am which was followed by their first meal. Nones at 2.00pm followed by weapons training, and Vespers at 6.00pm. Then they would have their second and final meal with Compline at 8.00 or earlier depending on the season and length of days.

As part of his Latin Rule physical relations with women were forbidden, although married men could be allowed to join the Order if their wives consented. Homosexuality was forbidden. Because hygiene was important (a healthy mind in a healthy body), every Templar was given changes of underwear – although they did have to ask their Commander for permission to have a bath – but not too frequently in case this weakened them.

What was striking was that Bernard also laid down a specific requirement on all Templar Knights to make obedience to Bethany, which was the home of Lazarus and his sisters Mary and Martha.

In his sermons on the Canticles of Canticles (the Song of Songs), Bernard equates the bride of the song symbolically with the church and with the soul of each believer. The prototype he selects to illustrate this 'Bride' of Christ is Mary the sister of Lazarus who later anointed Jesus feet with nard and dried them with his hair. But he also said repeatedly that Mary of Bethany was the same as Mary Magdalen.

So was Bernard, despite the austerity of his Rule, more attune to the feminine – sacred or otherwise – than he might have been able to say in that era? And how did it affect his beloved Templars?

***

Sometimes, as you explore new areas, it is the little things you notice in the distance that stay in the memory. You create a mental bookmark in which you say: *I must go back there.* Margaret and I have done this in relation to church steeples rising from the misty landscape, castle ruins, old pubs, unusual clumps of woods, isolated hills, and even old lighthouses, water towers and once, on a hilltop on the Isle of Wight, a phone mast. From the base of the latter, at sunset, she was entranced by glimpses to the west of Tir n'an Og, the Land of Eternal Youth. For myself I was made ill by what I imagined were the microwave radiations from the mast. I'd go again just for the views, but with a tin-foil hat next time.

Likewise, it is often something *said* in passing that sticks in the mind over the years and that you wish you could return to and explore. Odd words said in striking ways that makes you wish you had stopped the flow and asked for more details. Sometime in the 1990s I was in Seattle staying with my pal Laura Jennings-York, a heavy duty and utterly delightful magus of a group there. She herself was yarning, and she mentioned some scrying that she had done with one of my oldest magickal pals Dolores Ashcroft-Nowicki, into either a dark bowl of liquid or dark mirror, I can't remember which. I never thought to ask the whys and wherefores of the Work, but in essence they were peering toward a Templar source from the early days of the Order. And when the contact was made Dolores exclaimed:

'But there are *women* in there!'

I should have stopped Laura then and there and drained her of that particular memory. Instead I was too busy showing off again: pointing out that her ceremonial *athame*, or witch's dagger, was actually a British commando dagger, devised by Messrs Fairbairn and Sykes who were formerly of the Hong Kong police, until recruited to teach their unique skills of unarmed combat during the Second World War.

What a conversation killer *that* was. What an idiot *I* was. I can't use the excuse that I was young and didn't know better. I must have been wearing that Templar's iron helmet with the narrow visor even then, without knowing. The modern word 'knob-head' springs to mind.

***

In fact women were part of the Order right from the start, but it seems only recently that historians have mused: *Why didn't we see that?* Women were admitted during the first decade of the Order and may even have been allowed active service, hence legends of the fighting Daughters of Tsion. A legitimate branch known as the Teutonic Order, which survived the suppression, formed at least one female monastery in 1305, the 'Abbey des Camaldules de Saint Michel de Lemo'. It is recorded that its Abbess Agnès took Templar Vows and was admitted by a Prior from Venice.

So the Order seemed to recognise women as equal to, but venerably different from, their male counterparts, yet all serving in balance as Brothers and Sisters. Call me old fashioned but that's how I think it should be. While they may not have been practising 'Sacred Sex' within their priories, at least the Templars were not as rigidly anti-women as popular histories have supposed. Marriage was regarded as wholesome and necessary. Even the Catholic Church itself did not insist upon celibacy until the 1500s.

On actual admission to the Order the initiate took an oath to 'God and the Lady St Mary', this being an almost coded reference to the Magdalen. Or else to 'God and Our Lady' or 'God and the Blessed Mary'. If absolution were ever needed for any perceived iniquity then the words were: 'I pray to God that he will pardon you your sins as he pardoned them to St Mary Magdalene and the thief who was put on the cross.' Throughout its existence the priests of the Order, rather like military chaplains today, served by the authority of the *Damedieu*, which specifically referred to the feminine aspect of God - again was a clear reference to Mary Magdalene.

At the start of this project I wondered whether the almost adjoining churches of Alton Priors and Alton Barnes actually catered for two slightly different kinds of Christianity. Although the latter is now dedicated to St Mary the Virgin it seems that in its earliest times it was simply known as St Mary's - 'the Virgin' being added much later.

Only a few miles across the fields in Woodborough is the church of St Mary Magdalen and although this is the product of the 19th Century there is proof that two previous churches have existed on this site, the first during the reign of Richard I, the Lionheart, and warrior of the Third Crusade. Perhaps the naming and renaming of these two small churches hint at other battles that have gone on within the quiet fields of Wiltshire.

'Following the myth' as I am determined to do, what I will speculate is this: the church of St Mary at Alton Barnes was (perhaps covertly) dedicated to the Magdalen; or else that its connection to the Templar church of All Saints next door was so obvious that no-one needed to specify. Later, in relatively modern times when the Magdalen was regarded askance and 'the Virgin' added to purify the place, some modern worshippers with Templar sympathies (and they do exist, still[1]) decided to dedicate the church in nearby Woodborough as if to say: *We haven't forgotten!*

There is also the adjoining village of Stanton St. Bernard. The first part of its name is derived from *stan* and *tun,* meaning stone farm, and thus a nod toward all the sarsen stones used in walls, cobbled paths and buildings.

How 'St Bernard' came to be added is still debated today, and local historians feel it is either related to the Burden family or the Berners from Alton Barnes. They point out that, although St Bernard himself is portrayed in one of the church windows, the village name could not possibly refer to the actual saint. Yet the Benedictine Order had a long-standing presence in this immediate area, and if the Templars really did infest the adjoining villages then Stanton St. Bernard really must refer to the *eminence gris* behind the Order.

Later, I'll 'follow the myth' a little further and try to give the identities of the actual saints that were honoured both in All Saints at Stanton St. Bernard and Alton Priors itself: I don't believe their brief was for *all* the saints throughout Christianity, but more exactly all the four saints particularly venerated by the Templars.

***

Today is April 1st and also Easter Sunday. I'm only aware of the latter because all the shops are closed. If there is any sense of this being April Fool's Day then it's only in terms of the so-called 'Way of the Fool', as described in Mark Edsel's book of that name. He describes this Way as an independent path of initiation whereby the student can at different times study under many masters but not make any lifelong commitment to any one path, nor enter into vows of secrecy. I suppose I've always been on that path without realising, though I'm leery about his idea of Masters. (As I can't say too often, all the genuine Adepts I've known were, at heart, just ordinary folk with as many bewilderments and torments as the rest of us.) When I read Edsel's book I realised by Chapter 5 that he was inventing all these Masters he was meeting across the globe. For one thing they all had the same conversations, in the same tone, about astrology and architecture; for another, they were all insufferably boring. I've no interest in astrology and less in in sacred architecture. I never got the end of that book.

**

This morning, Margaret suggested that we go to Alton Priors and then picnic on Tan Hill. So, within a short space of time, we parked next to St Mary's church at Alton Barnes and made our way along the cobbled footpath across the fields to All Saints. If I were to novelise this moment to create atmosphere I would add crows and a black dog, but both really were present. The collective noun for crows is a 'murder' and there was certainly a huge murder of them – a positive mass slaughter - in the trees around. It has always been my totem bird and the sound of its *kraa* makes me tingle.

Ahead of us, crapping on the path, was an evil looking black dog of some sort. I am not fond of dogs but will make an exception for Jo's preternaturally aware little terrier. Usually I tell friends who own one that I am afraid of dogs, so as not to hurt feelings. That way they put their beasts outside and I can talk, and not have to pretend it's cute when it sniffs at my crutch and they end up insisting: *He won't hurt you!* Paddy eventually had to have her dog put down when it turned on someone.

Just saying.

'Go away,' I told the black dog in our path that day, but its owner called it from a distance and the route was made clear.

There are also three small turnstiles on the path, of a type I've never seen elsewhere, made of equi-armed crosses, one of them before a small bridge. I made sure that as I went through, each cross would turn in a clockwise direction. The stream below the bridge was crystal clear. If I've a tendency to see all stones as forgotten standing stones then I've a yen for thinking of all bridges across streams as Faery Bridges - links between one realm and another, enabling liminality. There's never any harm in asking for permission to cross and I did so then

As I stood in the area where the door had been, back against the stones, I am aware that the frame had been broken on my left-hand side and bits of it used for infill. I suppose this is something of a metaphor for all our lives in differing ways but I'll have to work that one through a bit more. I was aware of all sorts of niggling energies or perhaps entities that had been wanting my attention recently and keeping me awake at nights, including perhaps a Turcopole, who I will write about later.

After some time, we strolled across to the Broad Well that was especially fascinating to Margaret, as she has always had a thing about such places and an uncanny knack for finding lost ones. 'Well' is something of a misnomer in this case. It is more of pond from which a stream flows. When I first saw it with Paddy and Jo we had to climb over a fence and the famous bubbles from the ground were desultory to say the least. The second time I saw it with Margaret last year they were only slightly more vigorous. This time it was almost a

44

cauldron, and the sandy bed in various places was being churned up in flows and folds, ever expanding, ever collapsing, like watching a miniature creation of the universe.

The old Templar revenant that Paddy's friend saw beside me would have been at this same church, touched the same yew tree, looked down on this same turbulence, heard crows and seen the same ridges of hills before him curving into Goddess shapes. Someday I will have to give him a name, historical or otherwise, just to make sense of whatever message he might be trying to pass on.

Before we went I had an urge to find a small stone from this area. One was almost underfoot, sticking out of the soil, a sharpish piece of rock in striking black and white, like the colours of the Beausant, the Templar battle flag. I asked permission to take this stone but left some gold (a pound coin) in its place, and it is on my desk before me as I write.

The weather turned sour then so we gave up on the Tan Hill picnic and came home, after which I gave my stone a guided tour of our little home and made it welcome. I dare say I'll come back to that also, and the use of our wands another time.

Thinking about the day later, and the places we visited, I realise I tend to take it for granted that everyone knows about the various sites in this ancient area. So perhaps I'd better sketch some of the places that our notional Templars would have known when they served here…

The Great Ridgeway, alongside of which the Templars maintained a preceptory, was an ancient track running along the high ridges of hills. It is unpaved but hard ground suitable for travelling on in all weathers. It stretches 85 miles from our church at Alton Priors to Ivinghoe Beacon near Tring, Buckinghamshire. It has been a major route for 5000 years for travellers, farmers, and armies. During Saxon and Viking times, it provided a useful track along which to move soldiers into the realm known then as Wessex. In later periods, the route would have been utilised by drovers, moving animals to market and Templars moving in their mysterious ways.

I would argue that it was also something of a Sacred Way, perhaps a pilgrimage route every bit as important as the much heralded one toward the shrine of the apostle Saint James the Great, in the cathedral of Santiago de Compostela in north-western Spain. The Ridgeway starts off within spitting distance of Avebury's Bronze Age stone circle which is one of the largest

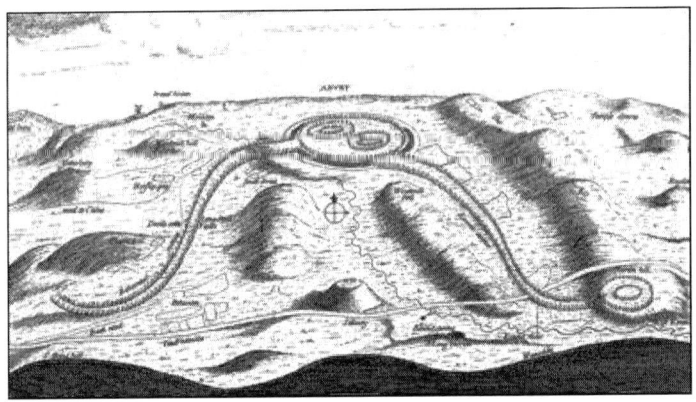

prehistoric monuments of this type in Europe and a dowser's paradise. Adjoining that is Silbury Hill, the largest man-made hill in Europe, that some have felt is a Star Gate. Further north is White Horse Hill in Uffington, the oldest hill-figure in Britain, dating to approximately 3000 years ago. It is said that if you stand on the eye of the dragon, turn three times and make a wish it will come true: though always with the proviso of being careful of what you ask for because… you might be unlucky and get it. If my fellow traveller has no idea what that means, then I can only say you are very young. I did stand on the eye, although this is not allowed. I was so battered at the time that I needed help from somewhere. I have to say that I made a very careful wish and it did come true.

Then there is Wayland's Smithy, a Neolithic burial mound some 5,000 years old. (Stonehenge, incidentally, is a mere 4000 years old.) It was named that by the Saxons who must have been in some awe of it, as Wayland was a Saxon smith god. It was believed that Wayland had his blacksmith's forge in the burial chamber. Paddy told me that one morning at dawn she had heard the sound of someone bashing metal inside but didn't explore. (I didn't believe her then and still don't. She could be a bit of a rascal, like all the best magicians, which is why I loved her.)

And not forgetting the Dragon Hill, believed to be where St. George killed the beast. The grass on the top of the hill has been worn away, and legend has it that it no longer grows where the dragon's blood seeped into the ground.

Plus some hollow stone through which, apparently, King Alfred blew and summoned his armies to drive out the heathen. I've forgotten the details of that one but I'd like to have a go myself.

And then there is…

The Wansdyke, which crosses the Ridgeway above Alton Priors. This is an impressive linear earthwork, consisting of a ditch and bank running approximately east-west, for some 40 miles that was probably built during the 5th or 6th century. No-one can agree as to whether it was created by the Romano-Britons as a defence against the marauding West Saxons, or as a means of controlling locals and travellers along the Ridgeway. The name is a corruption of Woden's Dyke, given by Anglo-Saxons who themselves probably had no idea as to its origins or purpose. Some have opined that because the ditch itself was formed by the exposed chalk, that it would glow in the starlight of the unpolluted skies. Others, less convincingly, that it was filled with water and used as a simple canal centuries before the modern ones in this area were even imagined.

***

As the Wiltshire poet and nature mystic Richard Jeffries wrote a century and a half ago, the hills of this county are 'alive with the dead'. They certainly are. I used to wonder if the Templars were drawn here because they had intuitive perceptions of the Earth energies radiated by the ancient sites and circles. Now I simply think that because there are so many of these surviving even today, despite massive destruction by farmers, builders, town and road makers, that no matter where they planted themselves a circle or henge or barrow or sacred well would be nearby.

With so many people passing this way, on all sorts of levels, over thousands of years, it's hard in my brooding state to focus on the great Goddess that lies just in front of me on which the White Horse of Alton Barnes prances rather like a tattoo. Fortunately, I got a little help in visualising Her.

I mentioned earlier about the Library Angel. All writers who have heard this term will confirm the extraordinary ways in which exquisitely relevant knowledge can be flung into their path in the local library.

Although I suppose that these days the same thing happens via Google. When I went on that crucial day trip with Paddy and Jo in 2001 it was the former who told me to stop the car so she could point out the landscape Goddess.

'Where?' I asked, because I couldn't see it at all.

'Well you have to use a *little* imagination!' was her somewhat testy reply.

It was only recently that the Library Angel flung a book into my hand that made Paddy's observation crystal clear and showed me that here again something had been hiding in plain sight, just like the women amid the Templars.

The book was *Legendary Landscapes – Secrets of Ancient Wiltshire Revealed* by J.D. Wakefield. The author, about whom I know nothing and cannot track down, was not enlightened by any arcane society of men wearing sashes and badges and having basket meals together. In the first paragraph he told how in 1996 he had sat down in the hollow centre of the ancient female yew tree in the churchyard of All Saints, at Alton Priors, and thought about the folk belief that yew trees extend their roots into the mouths of the buried dead, soak up their secrets and transform them into 'whispers to be blown loose from the foliage into the wind'. If your nape hairs aren't prickling with excitement on reading *that* then get off my horse.

Wakefield was then inspired to discover the sleeping goddess in that area of the Pewsey Vale, and writes:

> When the hills are viewed from the east the secret is revealed, for the hills and Neolithic sites built onto them create the impression of a recumbent woman who has just given birth. The natural jutting spur from Walker's Hill is an elongated neck. Milk Hill and Walker's Hill form two huge breasts, and the barrows that crown them create a nipple effect. Knap Hill is a pregnant belly, the unusual bank running down is the umbilical cord, and a low bowl-shaped barrow alongside the bank is a swollen navel…This gigantic 'woman' part natural, part artificially made seems to depict a goddess figure who has just given birth into the field below – the East Field.

Why didn't I find this before? I wondered, when the book came to me. Fortunately, I had brought it with me today and showed it to Margaret, as, like myself, she just couldn't make out the goddess figure when we had driven past it on previous trips to see the extraordinary Dee Banton at the other end of the Vale.

'Of course!' she said, using considerably more imagination than I had done with Paddy.

***

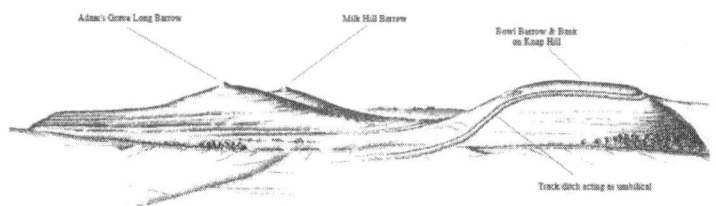

Adapted (some might say stolen) from J.D. Wakefield's far better drawing. I've done my best to find him but with no luck.

For the past few nights I have gone to sleep while visualising myself with the back to the door again. I know that sometime in the future I will actually face the door and visualise it opening, but I don't know enough yet. In fact, whoever is on the horse behind me can do that for themselves. You don't have to visit places in the flesh to get essences from them: you create them within you, where they exist all along. I have known American magicians, in America, doing group work involving Glastonbury Tor. They placed a photograph of it before the group, closed their eyes, used a few simple attunement techniques, and let their minds travel. This is not astral projection, by the way. In fact, I'm not sure exactly what it is, to be honest. But somehow it works.

Once or twice during my nights before the Door, if I might call it that, even before we went on our picnic, I visualised myself wearing the white outfit of a Templar knight to see if it might create a burst of recognition or acceptance from whoever lies within. In each case nothing happened and I simply dropped off to sleep and had the most ordinary non-Templar dreams. I've never been one for receiving spectacular visions though it does seem that the seeds I plant on the edge of sleep eventually take root and grow.

As I lay and brooded, Margaret reading another bloodthirsty thriller next to me, I did wonder what our Templar might have felt if he had stood there and looked north. Even today, in this area, there is a minimum of street lighting. Then, in the years before 1307, he would have had a complete Dark Sky experience: the infinitude of stars, meteors, and the Milky Way, which many modern town dwellers have never glimpsed except in photographs, often imagining it is seen only in exotic climes when actually it is always up there, above them, here and now, if you get the place and darkness right.

Would he feel homesick? – he may not be a native of Britain. Would he have been based at the Templar preceptory a few miles north along the Ridgeway to do his daily business? Would he be lonely? Would he be lovesick?

But from my own present point of view, would he have mused upon the Goddess in the hills before him, as I've increasingly been doing? He would certainly have been aware of the local beliefs and rites involving the latter, some of which persisted in corrupted forms right up until the 20th Century and are being resurrected by modern pagans now. In fact at that time he would have seen the massive complex of standing stones at Avebury at their intact and awesome height, before people in the Victorian era started using them for houses and barns, or the farmers levelled them for their fields. You don't need to have much intuition to be aware, even today, of the cosmic and fundamentally sexual interplay between the Sun, Moon and Stars that enacts itself within the complex, as revealed by the inspired researches of modern astro-archaeomystics, to coin an awkward term. Then, he couldn't *not* have been aware.

Here in the 21st Century the area around is littered with the remains of standing stones, ruined/forgotten circles, sacred ponds and wells, long and round barrows filled with the remains of ancestors and their guardian spirits who won't leave. In *his* day, that landscape would have been intact and overwhelming.

I do think there is such a thing as what Dion Fortune described as 'Heavenly Homesickness': a deep yearning to return to an inner source. Plus I think there is also a Heavenly Lovelorn-ness, to create a clumsy term, in which the seeker can pine for something in the way of a spiritual Beloved. It was Krishamurti who wrote: 'I would show you how I have found my Beloved, how the Beloved is established in me, how the Beloved is the Beloved of all and how the Beloved and I are one so that there can be no separation either now or at any time.'

Although I'm not a follower of Krishnamurti I think his own search for this inner essence of the essentially feminine Beloved is deeply moving. I think that St Bernard with his passion for Black Madonnas, Mary Magdalen, Mary, Mother of God and the secret, Sacred Feminine echoes this. And when it came to the ordinary Templar, welded into his vows as much as his armour, obeying the strict rules of the Order, he would often have become so horny that he would wonder if it was all worth it. From imagining, when the joined the Order, that he was part of an elite about to get just spiritual rewards, he would envy the sight of the simple women, living simple lives, going to the Broad Well to fill their pitchers. I think that 'my' knight would have felt somewhat cheated, somewhat foolish. He might well have echoed Jung's knights and cried to himself: *I have joined*

53

the Order of the Poor Knights and found not that which I sought.

Among the curious carvings on the walls on the dungeons in Chinon where some Templars were held after the suppression, and also in the caves at Royston there is one that stands out and may be useful. It is the hand with a heart on the  palm. It seems to be symbolic of charity as well as mercy and has been used by later groups as diverse as the Shakers and Oddfellows. Whoever carved this has known love at some level and has not given it up and is still willing to offer it. I think we'll come back to that one later.

***

Still brooding before the Door, though, and looking toward the Goddess, I now want to use our Templar's eidolon to explore the exact place on the Alton Goddess that J.D. Wakefield would come to identify nearly 700 years later as Her actual *yoni,* to use a genteel word.

That will be the site of our next trip.

This might be a steep climb and get very hairy. Hang on at the back. …

Chapter 4

Creating Ghosts

We drove along the Vale of Pewsey today with the aim of climbing Knap Hill and walking along to the triangular-shaped area that joins it with Golden Ball Hill. This, it was felt, was the *yoni* of the Goddess, though I much prefer the old word *cunt.*

I can feel the rider behind me squirm at the use of that, but it might be because of upbringing and inherited attitude. Mathew Hunt – and you might want to google this - argues that the origins of the word can be traced back to the Proto-Indo-European 'cu', one of the oldest word-sounds in recorded language, and is an expression profoundly associated with femininity, forming the basis of 'cow', 'queen' and 'cunt'. He also adds that, today, it is a primary example of the multitude of tabooed words and phrases relating to female sexuality, and of the modern misogyny inherent in sexual discourse. While on a similar tack it was Michael Dames in his ground-breaking book on the goddess of Silbury Hill, who argued that the nearby River Kennet owes its name to the same word and points out that Gropecunt Lanes were common in many English towns in the 13th Century and later. Certainly our Templar (and I will name him soon), would not have blinked twice on hearing it.

In fact my wife, who is not fazed by this wonderful and rebarbative term, used it to describe the driver of an Audi who overtook us at ridiculous speed on a bend of the narrow road as she drove us toward the goddess in the hills.

'But what has this to do with Templars?' she asked, as we approached the pregnant belly that is Knap Hill.

Well, I accept that the Order was an expression of, and outlet for, what some have termed the Great European Heresy: the covert worship of the Goddess as an equal to the God, as expressed through (among others) Mary Magdalen and John the Baptist, involving powerful undercurrents of Sacred Sexuality. But our Templar, standing with his back to the door, would have found himself looking out toward something infinitely older, yet perpetually present: the Goddess in the Land – the Goddess which *is* the Land. Such awareness, however nominal, would have had a troubling effect. The area around him would have been thrumming with local ceremonies of barely concealed 'horniness' that honoured deities older than anything from Outremer, however heretical. The very church behind him would have its All Saints' Day every November 1, which throughout the pagan world was also known as Samhain, celebrated from 31 October to 1 November. In both traditions, Christian and Pagan, this is a day dedicated to the cheerful dead, both personal and ancestral.

Thinking of the distraught Templars who crowded into Jung's house that day and the release he offered them, I wonder if I should tell 'our' Templar: *Your Holy Land is not Holy to me. What you see in front of you, with your back to the door, has everything you seek.*

As we approached the range of hills we could see that the sky above the area we hoped to penetrate was exploding with paragliders, like a cloud of rainbow midges, taking advantage of the sunny day and the stiff breeze. No matter how I try, I still can't find any spiritual metaphor (perhaps involving spirits of Air and Earth?) to make that sight part of our quest.

'Let's not go there today,' said Margaret and I agreed. I'm not good with crowds. And crowds of people with parachutes and wearing lycra would be a cruel and unusual punishment. Instead we drove onto the nearby Martinsell Hill which, I am fairly sure, our Templar would never have climbed or even noticed.

***

The hill itself is one of the oldest hill-forts in the county, if not England. It rises disturbingly steeply from the floor of the Vale but proved rather easy to climb. In Victorian times they would have a great fair on Palm Sunday. Boys used to slide down the hill on the jawbones of horses; men from the neighbouring villages would settle their grudges by fighting. From the top, in every direction, there are clear views of the countryside, as far away as the huge spire of Salisbury Cathedral some 25 miles to the south. And to the north/north-east, the Ridgeway itself, and the area where the Templars had their preceptory.

Sometimes, there is the need for all of us to align ourselves with the primary directions. It is a simple enough process, which can have surprising results.

In the old days of the chunky plastic monitors for the new-fangled pc, you would need to de-gauss the screen at regular intervals when it got too fuzzy and twisty. Something to do with decreasing or eliminating a remnant magnetic field, apparently. You simply had to press a button on the monitor and it would hiss and fizz a while before the screen cleared. Hulls of ships had to be regularly de-gaussed during the War in case they set off hidden mines. And there is certainly a metaphor in *that* one: we all have periods in our lives when we're sailing along quite happily but suddenly seem to set off mines without even knowing they are there.

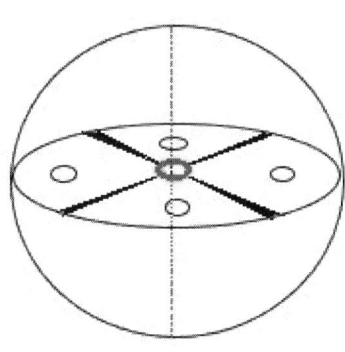

Now get off the back of the horse, take your helmet off and that horrible armour, and simply be still. Visualise yourself next to us on the top of Martinsell Hill or just settle down in your own room where you're reading this and align yourself to the directions. Stand facing north, if that appeals, in the centre of your own spiritual cross pattée. Be aware of the Four Quarters: Sunrise, Noon, Sunset and Night. And add to them the remaining three directions of: Above, Below and Within.

Just spend some time feeling yourself to be part of this universe, aligned with its workings. Later, I will suggest a list of correspondences to fit into the Quarters for extending this and working your own simple rites. At the moment, still travelling, we don't want to take on board too much weight.

I first read of this simple arrangement in William G. Gray's brilliant *Magical Ritual Methods* when I was a teenager and his words on this are still relevant:

> We now have a workable nucleus for a Magical Cosmos which is capable of indefinite extension… [There] is absolutely nothing in the entire field of Consciousness which cannot be co-related harmoniously with it at some angle or another. It is impossible to over-estimate the

importance of this. The creator of such a Cosmos becomes a God in his own right, however minor this might be relative to other units of Deity. To such a one, everything makes sense, becomes true, fits in perfectly somewhere and works at its best. They become healthy ('Whole-thy') happy and harmonious beings, balanced at all points and rotating (living) truly to their principles of construction.

But that's enough de-gaussing for now. Those of you who don't know about William G. Gray might want to do some research. In this the Aeon of Google, the crowned and conquering child of the search engines, you can do this sort of thing on your phones.

***

What has this to do with Templars you might ask? Nothing. But then my intention has never been to do one of those all-embracing Idiots Guides that appear on every bookshelf. As I said earlier I'm curious as to what the revenant who stood next to me in Paddy's sitting room wanted.

Was he – is he – some fragment of a past life crying out for attention? I doubt it. I've always had a different take on 'past' lives anyway. Besides, I've never had any feel for this period, never once thought I might have been a Templar knight, sergeant, or general bottle-washer in a Preceptory or Commanderie.

Was he – is he – an earthbound spirit who has somehow been attracted to me in hopes of getting release? I don't know. I've never been quite psychic enough to communicate with such beings in the way I've seen others do. And believe me that is not false modesty on my part.

Also I believe that inner contacts, at any level, should always be a two way event. If gods or goddesses or 'higher' beings make contact with anyone, it is with the understanding that they want to learn from you as much as you from them. If there is anyone still on the back of my horse after this, they must realise that the days of knee-bending worship are over. Would you want anyone bowing before *you*? The Goddess in the Land wants you to work with Her, not make nice, reverential noises. The same is true of the secret deities that may have been behind the Great Heresy, which the writers Picknett and Prince trace all the way back to Isis and Osiris.[1]

So my words to the lost and lonely Templar are also: *Take what you need from me, but also give me back in equal measure, in terms of learning.*

It was while we were atop this hill, opening the flask of tea and starting on our sandwiches that I worried a little about the name 'Giant's Grave'. Local reports seem to refer to the whole hill as the Giant's Grave, but this is a common term throughout the southwest for various long barrows. I don't think that larger than normal bones have been excavated from any of them. There was one long ridge of earth up there that, to me, was 'long barrow-ish' but I've already confessed my tendency to project all sorts of nonsense onto the very the ordinary. It made me realise then that the Giant – whether the hill itself or that mound – had no name and no story. Perhaps the Giant was the seen as the consort/lover of the Alton Barnes goddess?

But if this big, strapping mound of earth-laddishness had no name that anyone can remember or create, then neither had my Templar.

In Ancient Egypt the concept of the *ren* was crucial to the soul's existence, and it is no less so today, wherever you are as you read this. Egyptians believed that the soul would live for as long as the person's birth-name was spoken, It is their essence, their experiences, and their entire life's worth of memories. If I wanted to communicate with the person sharing my journey then I would, eventually, have to learn their name in order to do so effectively.

So I will give our man a name now, and explain on a later stage of our ride how and when it came to me, some time ago. I will call him:

Ancuellos.

***

I suppose that what I'm doing is creating a literary Avatar again. I say 'again' because I did this for my grandfather George Matthew Richardson M.M. & Bar, when I wrote *Geordie's War,* as means of understanding what he did and why, how he might have felt, what he needed to do to survive the Great War and all its horrors. In fact, just using his name in that sentence I am giving power to the *ren.* Ancuellos might not be the actual name of 'our' man but we have to get a grip somewhere.

In the late 20th Century magicians would use the term 'Telesmic Image' to describe their means of contacting entities on the inner planes. If, for example, they would want to make contact with the Archangel Michael (or Horus, or Arthur or Cernunnos) they would create an actual image of such in their mind's eye and use it in their meditations. As William Gray advised me many years ago:

> When you feel able to shut your eyes and 'call up'
> or 'evoke' a clear image of Michael in your mind

– do so, and [see] what comes through. It will only answer you from the information you have 'banked' with yourself, *but* the way that information comes out and the new knowledge you gain from this should have come from the 'Michael-Concept' in our Cosmic, (or as Jung would have said: 'Collective') Consciousness.

When I had some doubts about this he later added:

Yes, why didn't you try and make your Figures stand on their heads? Have a go at this, and when they refuse to obey silly or undignified suggestions, you'll know their 'Inners' are taking up the Images you obligingly made for them to occupy.[2]

In this context it is worth looking up details of that famous 'Philip experiment' in 1972, conducted by the mathematician A. R. G. Owen and overseen by psychologist Dr. Joel Whitton within the Toronto Society for Psychical Research. Their group created an entirely fictional character whom they called Philip Aylesford, deciding that he was born in 1624 in England, had an early military career, was knighted by the age of sixteen then had a glamourous few years including a tragic love affair with a witch before committing suicide in 1654. After building up the persona they then attempted to communicate with 'Philip' through traditional séance. In due course the group began to feel a presence, table vibrations, breezes, unexplained echoes, and rapping sounds which matched responses to questions about Philip's life. In due course, as he became stronger, he was able to start moving the seance table and was apparently capable of levitating it. Sitters reported seeing a mist over the table that would move across the room when someone entered, as if it was greeting them. He was also capable of dimming the lights on command.

They never quite got beyond the contents of their group mind (as Gray described above) but they certainly created *something*.

Taking this experiment somewhat further, however, I have known a group of senior magicians who used the figures from Tolkien's *Lord of the Rings* to create telesmic images aimed at linking with the Elvish, faery realms, and who did so with great effect.

So I suppose that what I've been doing is much the same, and will carry on. I will use the image of an old Templar, create a character for him like the Toronto group did for 'Philip', pack it with as much knowledge and energy as I can, then see if it/he links with the Templar egregore in the inner planes and brings through *new* knowledge and insights as Bill Gray insisted. Of course I might end up with nothing more than ego on my face but that has never worried me.

***

Our Templar, Ancuellos, doesn't seem to be wearing chain mail in my mind's eye. I suppose I want him to be comfortable, and it wouldn't really be needed at this time, in the heart of the Wiltshire countryside. Let's give him a shorn head and a full red beard. We know that underneath everything he wore a simple woollen shirt, woollen breeches and leggings, though in the heat of the Outremer he could change to linen underclothes. On top of that he is wearing an ankle length, belted and hooded, white tunic with tight fitting sleeves, over which he could fling a loose sleeveless white mantle. No decorations were allowed except the Templar cross over the left breast. We don't need to see him with a helmet: we want to see what he is thinking.

This is a simple and rather perfect Telesmic Image that will start to imbue itself with knowledge – our own knowledge – immediately.

Be aware, also, that in his background he would have been allowed 4 horses and a squire, and he would have been issued with a lance, sword, a mace, dagger, a bread knife and a shield.

***

If 'Philip' was given a faux-historical background to create substance, what would be the structure of Ancuellos' day-to-day Order? That is, what sort of inner world might he inhabit that parallels the historical one?

Each Templar belonged to a monastery-castle known as a Preceptory, or Commandery with its own master, responsible to his Provincial Master or Grand Prior, and ultimately to the Grand Master. The hierarchy would go like this…

The Grand Master was the supreme authority, answerable only to the Pope. They served for life. Several Grand Masters were killed in battle, showing that they were in it for more than just the fancy dress.

The Seneschal was the right hand-man to the Grand Master. He also looked after many administrative duties.

The Marshal was in charge of war and anything that was related to it. In this sense he could be seen as the second most important member of the Order. He was allowed two squires, one turcopole and one sergeant. He had four horses at his command. An Under Marshal was in charge of the footmen and equipment.

The Standard Bearer was in charge of the squires.

The Draper was in charge of the Templar garments and linens who made sure they didn't get lax in their appearance. (This may seem medievalist to accord the Draper such high status, but in the World War II general Patton insisted that all his officers maintained the immaculate dress of the men in their command. His argument was that if a Lieutenant, say, could not make a private keep his uniform neat and his tie fastened properly, how could he expect the private to follow him when he was ordered into battle?) The Draper was allowed four horses, two squires, several tailors and one brother in charge of the pack animals who would carry supplies.

Then there is **The Beausant,** the Templar battle-flag. It is the simplest of black and white devices but flags in previous eras had importance that we can scarcely appreciate today. Until the 20th Century soldiers were willing to die to protect their flag – either national or regimental - from the enemy. Capturing the enemies' flag  could result in them losing heart and leaving the field. The

Beausant was carried into battle by a Marshal and protected by a chosen core of ten Knights. An attribute peculiar to the Templars is said to have been that, unlike any other combatant anywhere, they advanced upon their enemies in silence. Perhaps holding the flag between two poles so as to be unmistakeable during a still day and telling their opponents: *We're coming...*

According to the statutes of the Order, knights must always be aware of the flag's location on the battle field. If they became scattered or disoriented they were supposed to gather in a formation under the Beausant. If the Templar banner was not visible, then the knights headed towards the Hospitaller flag to carry on the battle. The Templars did not cease fighting until the Beausant left the field. Consequently, the struggle did not cease until the enemy was destroyed or the Templars were all killed.

This black and white flag, perhaps signifying a different kind of battle - between good and evil - was probably the most important symbol for each individual Knight Templar.

I'll come back to that symbolism later.

***

Can we place him in time to a particular year? Would it be disrespectful if I use the date of Sept 11 1307? After all, that's when I first discovered the cross pattée on the church 694 years later. I sometimes feel that Ancuellos was a troubled old chap, and while the mass arrests of the Templars didn't take place until Friday the 13th October, 1307, I sense a weariness and a worry about him.

In 1291, the last Crusader stronghold fell to the Muslims in Acre, which signified the end of the Crusades. This left the Templars without a military role and in a precarious situation. Many were upset that the knights were not fulfilling their military duties by going back to the Holy Land and renewing the fight. Instead they seemed to want to bask in their special privileges and enjoy vast wealth. The Order was no longer held in awe by 1307 and Ancuellos must have sensed that he was a stranger in an awkward land, with bad things approaching from all directions.

The drawings below are just stock images of Templars plucked from the internet. The one on the left is the legendary Jacques de Molay, last Grand Master who was burnt at the stake. The others are ordinary knights and wearing much the same uniform. In fact the latter doesn't seem to have changed much over the two centuries of the Order's existence, although the helmets became more sophisticated. I feel quite sure that they kept their hair short purely as a practical consideration when wearing helmets.

I worry about modern soldiers today and hope that more can be done to deal with Post Traumatic Stress Disorders. I think our Ancuellos has had a touch of this and probably yearns to join a group like the gentle Cathars in southern France, who we will yarn about later.

***

As I write this it is actually Friday 13th and I am holding my little 'templar stone' that has its own name. I'll go to sleep now with it under my pillow and hope for wild dreams. Time will tell whether our Telesmic Image of Ancuellos is going to get vivified by all this attention it's getting.

Chapter 5

Dreams and Earthbounds

Not exactly wild dreams last night. That is, I didn't see silent Templars riding into battle against the wily Saracen. Nor did I glimpse them manipulating the plasma energies of the Ark of the Covenant or communing with the severed head of John the Baptist and/or Jesus. As for their Holy Grail, they can keep it. But I did have a nice meeting with Prince Harry who invited me to his forthcoming wedding to Meghan Markle. He was very nice to me throughout the dream and we got on well. I used to have similar dreams about meeting his rather stiff father, various modern rock stars, and the great actor Laurence Olivier when he was still alive. None of whom I actually met in the flesh, you understand.

There is not one atom of belief within me which half-fancies that these individuals were coming to my dreams in their astral bodies in the way that spiritualist Guides would come to their mediums. I know that for me, when I dream of *soi-disant* 'celebrities', it is an attempt by my mind to bridge the gap that exists between normal consciousness and the supra-normal. These dream-figures, however glamorous, are also akin to Telesmic Images.

I know of a whole group of magicians from the 1920's and 30's[i] who used the images of various historical Lords Chancellors of Britain: Lord Eldon, Lord Erskine and the dreadful Thomas More (who punished those heretics that dared translate the Bible into English).

What was going on here, and how is it relevant to us?

Well, the title Chancellor is derived from *cancellarius,* namely one who is stationed at a doorway to introduce visitors, and also the King's chief secretary to whom petitions were delivered. He is thus a gate-keeper and guardian and technically 'higher' in status than anyone in parliament. And so the King or Queen, (who is the personification of the land and all its people), is reached via the Lord Chancellor. In a sense, the role is a connection between mortal and divine, between the common man and royalty. A direct link between the worldly and the spiritual.

I doubt if any magicians these days would find themselves using such historical figures, however potent they were in their day. But it is this concept of someone standing at the *doorway* that is important again. I have known other magicians quietly invoke Merlin when they cross certain boundaries or pass through relevant doors/gates/arches/portals with a quick inner *Hello!* Others from the Wiccan traditions, standing on the edges between field and forest, have invoked Cernunnos. Between land and sea, it might be Morgan le Fay who would come to mind. As with the injunction in *Field of Dreams*, build the doorway and they will come.

It is all to do with liminality, I suppose, which is something else my rider might want to look up after dismounting. There is an infinite universe of liminal beings out there – which is also in here. There are also liminal places that you can find or create for yourself. At the bottom of our little garden we try to make peace with whatever beings might be dancing there and I've regularly implored them not to hide my tools when I try, in my famously bodging way, to repair things.

So my dream of Prince Harry I took to be a kind of a nudge, or hint, that energies or entities on the other side might be amenable to making a connection. On the other hand, if I *did* get an invite to his wedding through the post, I'd be there in a flash.

***

Prince Harry apart, I think the stone under the pillow must have had some effect because later on that night I was troubled by a single word which has crept into my mind and stayed there like an ear-worm: Turcopole. Of course, I would have noticed it when first reading about the Templars but it meant nothing to me at the time. *Turcopole Turcopole Turcopole...* went the mantra, leading me at one point to go downstairs and google it.

It seems that turcopoles were hired by the Templars to act as a kind of tertiary cavalry. First came the knights themselves on the powerful beasts known as *destriers*; then came the sergeants with their lances and bows to tackle anything from the flanks; and then came the turcopoles on their smaller and faster horses, and wearing much lighter armour that often involved no more than a quilted jacket and a conical steel helmet.

Turcopoles were mercenaries. Historians today argue that they were of mixed Greek and Turkish parentage and were at least nominally Christian, but most may have been at least nominally Muslim. Those captured at the Battle of Hattin, in 1187, were executed at Saladin's order, as having betrayed Islam. In the barracks they were obliged to eat at a separate table from the knights and their sergeants. I doubt if they had much interest in the religious aspects of the Crusades or deep loyalties to their leaders: as long as they were paid adequately, they would fight. In fact, funding the turcopoles to boost the numbers of the

Crusader armies was where the greater cost of sustaining the Crusades came from.

Whenever I look at the Templars I cannot avoid taking a side-glance at Islam, and the influence it had upon them. Which is why my ears pricked up on seeing the 'Arabic' style of the doorway, and the leaflet inside the church that mentioned the Arabic numbers on the sundial, instead of the usual Latin, and the existence of the (alas Victorian) octagonal font. (However, I must point out to my fellow rider, clinging on behind, that as I am a life-long sufferer of impaired hearing, with British Sign Language as my second language, my ears 'pricking up' means nothing. Please feel free to dismount, stop the horse and challenge anything I might say.)

When the first Poor Knights first made their way around Outremer it wouldn't have been their ears pricking up they experienced, but their eyes opening wide. As Sean Martin noted in his book: '…one of the most important things in the development of the West was the discovery of the East, Arabic culture and science being far in advance of the West at this time.' The first Templars took off their (in comparison) primitive armours and soaked it all up.

When they arrived, it was into an era now recognised as the Islamic Golden Age which ran from the 8th to the 14th Century. The knowledge of physics, optics, mathematics, astronomy, biology, chemistry was beyond anything known in the West. Islamic medicine integrated, Roman, Persian as well as the ancient Indian traditions of Ayurveda. . Even the humblest Arab doctor understood how to use mould extract to create antibiotics for treating wounds. They were centuries ahead of the West in terms of commerce, travel, map-making, poetry and sacred architecture. Sean Martin adds that in Moorish

Spain the Templars came into contact with those who were adept in geometry, alchemy, and the Kabbalah. Idries Shah argued that they learned sacred, alchemical building design techniques from what he termed the 'Sufi Freemasons' of the al-Banna, and that they applied this wisdom back in Europe when they designed their preceptories and churches in the shapes of octagons, circles and domes. The ordinary Crusaders were just brutal thugs, but the Templars absorbed the concept of Chivalry and brought it back to Europe.

And then there were their contacts with the already legendary Assassins, a renegade order of knights that preceded the Templars. Their red and white uniforms may even have inspired the black and white flag, the Beausant. The two orders reflected each other in so many ways that enemies of the Templars back in the West whispered that they were the same. In fact the disastrous 2nd Crusade was seen to have failed because the Templars and Knight Hospitallers had adopted so many local customs that they had gone native.

All esoteric speculations apart, at very least it was well known that the Templars employed Muslim secretaries and that the Grand Masters wouldn't have anyone else.

There are many other aspects to the Templars' contacts with the mystical aspects of Islam, which are beyond my horse-ride at the moment. Intriguingly, it is believed that the very term 'sarsen' is a shortening of 'Saracen stone' which arose in the Wiltshire dialect. As mentioned earlier, Saracen was a common name for Muslims but came to be used for anything regarded as non-Christian, whether Muslim, pagan Celtic, or other. So our church of All Saints at Alton Priors is actually built upon Saracen stones, just as the West itself was built upon the Saracen learning.

Mainly I am wondering why the word *Turcopole* kept me awake so determinedly. I am not psychic enough to be able to say that an earth-bound spirit, forgotten by all and sundry, was trying to grab the reins of my horse, so to speak. Realistically, I think I was meant to take a little detour and by researching turcopoles find out, to my own amazement, just how much the Templars learned in Outremer. Yet in case it is something of the former, let us take our armours off now and relax while I trot into another yarn, 'following the myth' again…

***

Joan Grant is almost forgotten now, although I am sure she can be googled back into a quasi-life on any pc. She was the first to use the term 'far memory' to describe the ability to tune into past lives. There are thousands, perhaps millions of past life counsellors and seers now, but Joan was among the first. She died in 1989 at the age of 82. I always regret that I never made the trip to Pangbourne to meet her, although we corresponded slightly. I know she would not have any doubts about the reality or otherwise of any troublesome Turcopole.

It was not her stories about past lives which first gripped me, however, but a yarn of her own in her excellent autobiography *Time Out of Mind*. As a very young and very psychic girl she witnessed the body of a suicide in the New York subway, from which her father rushed her away. That night however, back in her hotel room, she found herself in spirit back on the subway platform, not as a young girl but as someone about eighteen. The spirit of the suicide became aware of her.

She tended him. Dealt with the battered bits of his form and saw him become young again. She helped dress him in new clothes. The surrounds of the subway changed as he changed, and now he was lying on spring grass under a willow tree. Then he yawned and opened his eyes, stretching his arms luxuriously toward the warm clear light. A girl in a pink dress came running along the path beside the bright water. He recognised her, called her name and scrambled to his feet, laughing with joy and running into the light....

And there is also the yarn told me by a cheery Mike Nowicki about his visit to Hadrian's Wall in Northumberland. The Wall was built by the Roman army on the orders of the emperor Hadrian following his visit to Britain in AD 122. At 73 miles long, it crossed northern Britain from Wallsend on the River Tyne in the east, to Bowness-on-Solway in the west, and was the north-west frontier of the Roman Empire for nearly 300 years. Mike became aware of numerous earthbound spirits there. They were young soldiers – legionaries – whose throats had been slit by wild Picts who had crept up with all the silence and skill of natural assassins; they hadn't a clue what had happened. They were still there, keeping guard, nearly 2000 years later.

'I had to become their commanding officer. I had to assume in my astral form the accurate style and manner of a military Tribune at least, so that I could outrank them and persuade them to depart.'

Once he had done that, he could appear before the earthbound wretches as Joan Grant had done before the suicide. He told them that he was now their commanding officer, that their duty was over and they could now go home. All they had to do was think of someone they loved, who would welcome them. Once that connection was made they were able to break free of that dank, cold realm and go joyously, into their light.

Not too long ago I did similar for a handful of souls at Hill 60, in Flanders, although I had to spend several weeks before my compulsive visit in researching the uniform and manner of General Haig, and kept a photograph of him on my desk-top. On a drizzly day near Ypres, before that disturbingly small but incredibly bloodied hill, something 'Haig-like' descended on me as I summoned them to 'Stand To Arms'. Several surprised Tommies appeared, including one bewildered German. 'Haig' told them that they had done their duties, and done them right well; that the War was over and everyone was at peace. He advised them to think of their wives, parents, girlfriends, children, friends or even just beloved pets, and then head toward that door that was opened behind them upon the command: 'Dismissed!'

They went, and so did General Haig. And let me tell anyone reading this: what the Brits call the 'Blackadder Version' of the officers and conflicts in the First World War is almost completely wrong.

***

I'll confess that I did spend some time acting 'as if', with respect to my notional turcopole. I acted 'as if' he really was an earthbound spirit, even if he/it was little more than an astral shell. The rider behind me might like to use this in future in case he or she has to deal with similar.

So, making use of the yarns given above I sat alone one evening and lit a single candle. Beyond that I visualised him standing on the other side of it, using the imagery that can be plucked in abundance from the internet. As for myself I assumed the whole Templar vestments, but without the chain mail and uttered, quietly, the Order's motto: *Non nobis Domine, non nobis...* (which I'll come back to later). Then, basically, I told him that he had completed his work and more than fulfilled his obligations. He no longer needed to stay. He could go home. I also felt – absurdly perhaps – the need to visualise a large white horse for him, similar to that hill figure at Alton Barnes (which, incidentally, has a local ghost-life of its own even though it is a modern creation). I helped him mount the horse, advised him to think of all those people whom he had loved, and visualised him riding off into the West, where souls are said to go at death. Yet my little internal psycho-drama got stuck at that point, the loyal turcopole just wheeled and fretted and I suddenly realised why: to him, his true home was in the East. Once I adjusted that within my visualisation he galloped off with relish.

I am too old now to worry about anyone asking: *Did that really happen in any magickal sense? Was it not just a pleasant fantasy?* Quite simply I don't know. At very least it freed something within me and I was able to get some sleep afterward.

If my yarns exasperate then find your own horse...

Chapter 6

*And... **Faery**?!*

During my long and satisfyingly varied life I've been enviously aware of numerous best-sellers in which the author travels to the ends of the earth to find teachers/groups/occult secrets/ Ascended Masters etc. only to find that they were on his own doorstep all along. I could have saved them all a fortune in travel expenses if they'd just written to me and enclosed a stamped and self-addressed envelope. I suppose that if the Trickster element that often accompanies my own work energises itself, then I will experience the reverse: despite scouring every millimetre of my doorstep, that which I'm seeking will be found on the other side of the world.

I won't go. You can mutter behind my back all you want about Mountains and Mohammed. To me, Templardom is a state of mind and can be accessed from an apartment in Chicken Leg, Ohio as easily as any physical site in the present world.

Since I started this project I've made a list of places that I want to visit in order to: have a picnic; understand the Templars; make sense of why they have been bothering me. They are all relatively (and deliberately) local: a mere horse-ride in fact. The furthest is to the east, being Temple Church, the original headquarters of the Order in London. This is 116 miles away, easily reachable via a leisurely train with its buffet carriage and dodgy sandwiches. Then, within my county of Wiltshire, we will drive to (as near as we can) Temple Rockley and the Glory Ann ponds off the Ridgeway. A little to the west of me and 30 minutes by the same train is the ruined Temple Church in Bristol, within walking distance of Temple Meads station. The latter now has no trace of Templars whatsoever, other than via its name, though you can get the same dodgy sandwiches at the same exorbitant price. And further to the northwest, in Herefordshire, we really must explore the very odd churches at Kilpeck and Garway, no more than 61 miles easy drive. We'll try to stumble upon a Bed and Breakfast place for that trip and hope that the landlady is perhaps a secret Adept of some Hidden Order.

There are other Templar sites in my immediate area that I already know about and I'm sure I'll find more, the deeper I dig. But – call me lazy or saddle sore – I don't want to ride too far. Thus I have no desire to travel to Scotland for the legendary Rosslyn, nor Balantrodoch, even though both would be easily reachable when I'm visiting family up north. Nor do I have any desire to go to the Templar heartlands in France, despite being a Francophile and doing my on-line Duo-Lingo lessons faithfully every day. (A small pop-up Owl has appeared on my screen telling me I'm now 63% fluent and must continue. I'm not sure I could actually order a meal over there though.)

Instead, the one place I really must go to soon, is St Mary's Church at Orchardleigh, in Somerset. That one really is almost on my doorstep, though it seems to have been enwrapped in an invisibility spell for most of my life in this area. I'll yarn about that one in a moment because this is where I picked up the name Ancuellos.

Meanwhile, I'll admit that I've already made an abortive and somewhat disastrous pilgrimage of sorts to the first on the list: the original Temple Church in London.

Although I had checked and re-checked the opening hours on-line, when I got there the great gates to the north and south of the huge complex (which includes the Inns of Court) were locked and remained so. The day had started brightly but as I approached the rain poured down, monsoon-like. I rather hoped that by persisting, despite being soaked to the skin, then the inner watchers within the Order might approve my commitment. Not a chance. So I spent a couple of hours in Costa Coffee, read all the newspapers, scribbled some Timeless Prose in my A4 notebook (fine-tipped biro and right page only, the left being used for additions or corrections), tried twice more at both gates then went back to the gloomy hotel, defeated.

I mention the weather not because it is (supposed to be) an English obsession, but that there is a long tradition of inexplicable, explosive weather - torrential rain, gales, thunderstorms or lightning – whenever innocent archaeologists have excavated long barrows, for example, or erstwhile magicians did their stuff at ancient sacred sites. Quoting the adept Gareth Knight:

> We live, in other words, on the plane of effects. What causes these effects remains a matter for metaphysical conjecture. Just on occasion, it feels as if one might be a pawn in some other higher being's chess game. And the burst of bad weather might be the way by which some higher being announces Checkmate!'

I had none of that when we first went to St Mary's at Orchardleigh, probably in 2006, and I wasn't in search of anything beyond a healthy stroll in sublime countryside. I had overheard a chance remark by someone about the delightful route her walking group had taken to the church on the island in the lake. For some reason I assumed they had been on a cheap fight out to Croatia or somewhere unusual enough to host such a powerful combination.

'What lake, what island, what church?' I asked, somewhat idly.

'Near Frome.'

I was stunned. Frome is one of my favourite small towns in the world and twenty minutes from where we live. I fact I've often banged on about how in two generations time (if the world survives) youngsters will be talking about the very unusual energies that flow through Frome – probably via St Katherine – and that Glastonbury will be seen for what it is. And please don't write to about this. Play devil's advocate and find out for yourself.

Over the years I have prided myself (and often bored people witless) on having explored *all* the highways and byways of my area. I'm the sort of sad individual who will pore over detailed local maps as others might do with newspapers or porn mags. I knew where all the footpaths, bridle ways and walking trails were across the counties of Wiltshire, Somerset and parts of Dorset. *What lake, what island, **what** church?* Yet when I got home, unfolded the requisite Ordnance Survey map, there it was: a gurt big lake that I never knew existed. How could I have lived in and explored this area for 35 years and never been aware of it?

Here is what the vicar wrote:

St. Mary's, Orchardleigh, enjoys the unique setting of being at the edge of a lake with a moat around the church. Hence it is often referred to

as 'the church on the island.' Its remoteness
means there is no electricity supply to the church
which means all our services are candlelit and
the organ has to be pumped by hand...

Exasperatingly (or perhaps fittingly given what I've said
about my dream-states) the church has increasingly
become the focus of 'celebrity' weddings because of its
unusual siting and atmosphere. It wasn't open on our first

visit and I knew
nothing about its
history but the long,
ancient slab
gravestone was so
similar to the ones
in the church of St
Mary at Limpley
Stoke that I was
determined to make a connection. As I said earlier, I'm
always happy to let myth over-ride reality. This grave was
probably as valid as Harry's wedding invite, but as I bent
and touched it I got the name *Ancuellos.*

Of course I've googled this many times over many
years, but learned nothing, found no links, no etymology.
At the time I just put it to the back of my mind because I
was so enchanted by the site and had no real sense of
Templar presence at that time. It was only years later that
I decided to use the name for the purposes of this book.

***

As I've been writing this, sitting in the corner of
Trowbridge's excellent library and looking out toward the
apple blossom trees around the car park, I'm find it rather

hard to move it along. It's as if my horse is so distracted by things around that it won't gee. I've just been sitting, staring, trotting on the spot, if horses can do that sort of thing.

'Is it the bloody Templars again?' asks my lovely wife when arrives from her gym and sees that I've got a thousand-yard stare.

'No, it's the bloody faeries…'

***

Forget Ancuellos for the moment. Get off the horse and remove that silly armour: the faeries don't like iron. Let me try to get through this next bit quickly.

I'm all too aware of a thousand tales whereby travelers in the Faery Realms make quick visits but, on returning, find that centuries have passed. I'm also aware of figures like Robert Kirk and Thomas of Ercildoune who were trapped in Faeryland. The denizens of these shimmering realms are enchanting, provocative, compelling, seductive, capricious, malicious and can be utterly powerful, tied in as they are with the Great Goddess. Many of them don't like humans at all.

Hold on tight while I whizz across the head-lights of this completely different energy source. Don't let them charm you. Don't look to the side, out the corners of your eyes…

***

Orchardleigh is a country estate in Somerset, approximately two miles north of Frome, and on the southern edge of the village of Lullington. Within the old estate are the Orchardleigh Stones on adjacent Murtry Hill, a probable neolithic burial chamber which was excavated in 1803 and 1804, when human bones and cremation urns were discovered. *The Modern Antiquarian* website quotes from an 1875 journal:

> The natives of the district to this day have a dread of passing near the stones except in broad daylight, as if there were still remaining the notion that they marked a place of burial, or perhaps of Pagan rites, in which Satan may have taken an active part.

The writer, posting as Rhiannon, also adds: 'The area is said to be haunted by a lady in white…a 'Lake Lady' more fairy than ghost…' She feels that the latter was actually from an area in Wales, and that the writer, a certain Ruth Tongue, got confused when writing about these stones and concludes: 'I suppose the only way to know is to find someone who's seen a white lady at Murtry Hill! Otherwise, it seems like the idea's stuck anyway.'

Two things here. Myths and their images do stick. They also grow. And yes I've actually met a woman who has not only seen a white lady here but communed with Her. One last yarn and then we'll ride out before the Sidhe start hosting.

***

Sadly, Sue Kearley died less than a year before writing this. A Frome lass born and bred, as I understand, she was also a wonderful seer but kept her talents well hidden. On a visionary journey which started in mist and emerged by the long barrow at Orchardleigh, she and her companion Ian met the guardian figure they called The Builder. After imparting unusual information about a liminal creature she thought of as the Firebird, he took them on a walk down to the island where the church is. The building there was less elaborate than it is now but inside they met the Woman in White and after a long communion involving details which don't concern us here, they returned to the long barrow, where it seemed that they were being watched by a faery troop on horses on the high ground which overlooks the modern road towards Frome. 'We sat by the barrow and looked at the sky and were shown a dragon-like bird flying out of Cley Hill which was lit up with the earth/dragon/energy. The fire-bird? Ian also saw kaleidoscopic patterns, as if sunlight was passing through the blue crystal.'

It seemed to her that there was a direct connection between the energies within the land and the pattern of the stars in the sky. I had a much earlier communication from her (frustratingly now lost) about her contact with the White Lady and the buried King, whom Sue accessed via the land beneath my notional grave of Ancuellos.

Has all this still got any real connection with Templars though? Well, you've yet to learn about Henry Newbolt and Bligh Bond, and I'll try to keep this is short as I can because I feel I'm in danger of falling down the rabbit-hole…

***

Orchardleigh House was the home of Sir Henry Newbolt

until his death in 1938, at the age of 76. He was a poet, novelist and historian, highly regarded in his day, and with a powerful role as government advisor, particularly on Irish issues. His two most famous poems in an era when poets were almost like rock stars were:

- **Drake's Drum**, in which he drew upon the legend that the drum owned by Sir Francis Drake will beat in moments of national crisis, and that the old sea dog will rise and save his country again as he did at the time of the Spanish Armada, when all seemed lost. Mind you, considering how shoddily he was treated by Elizabeth I, I wouldn't be surprised if he just stayed asleep.

- **Vitaï Lampada** which means 'the torch of life' and refers to how a schoolboy, a future soldier, learns selfless commitment to duty in cricket matches, ending in the once-famous line cried out by many young and desperate subalterns in the Great War: 'Play up! play up! and play the game!'

But he also wrote a novel, now long lost, called *Mordred*, and a very strange but highly influential and almost completely forgotten fantasy called *Aladore*, copies of which can still be downloaded free from the internet. In brief it is about Ywain, a bored knight who goes on a pilgrimage to seek his heart's desire. Following a will-o'-the-wisp resembling a child, he is led to a hermit dwelling in the wilderness, under whose instruction he lives for a time. Later, his quest takes him to the otherworldly city of Paladore where he meets and woos the half-fae enchantress Aithne, the daughter of Sir Ogier of Kerioc and the Sidhe-descended Lady Ailinn of Ireland. At the time of writing, there were very few books of this kind, and one critic described it as having a 'dreamlike chamber-music air of its own.'

Sir Henry was also a bit of a black sheep because

of his *ménage a trois*. His wife had a passionate lesbian affair (is that term still acceptable?) with her cousin and truest love Ella Coltman. In due course Sir Henry also became Ella's lover and the trio co-existed quite happily and without jealousy to the end of their lives. He is buried on the island, next to the lake, and I can't think of a better place.

I think I would have liked him.

Illustration from Aladore. You can use this as a gateway, incidentally.

***

But then there is Bligh Bond, who died in 1945 aged 71. In the little guide to St Mary's the very first paragraph states: "This small parish church was described by Sir Nikolaus Pevsner as 'exceptionally interesting" and by F. Bligh Bond as an architectural gem." The man himself has been described by Richard Coates as:

> English architect, architectural illustrator, ecclesiologist, colour photographic pioneer, archaeologist, in later life a psychical researcher, a devout if unorthodox Christian, a man of somewhat anti-establishment leanings

politically as well as religiously, and a prolific, indefatigable writer and lecturer. [1]

That's just the beginning. Of course, he is known to all Brits of my generation as the author of *The Gates of Remembrance* and *The Hill of Vision*, both published in 1914, which he claimed were the result of psychic guidance from dead Glastonbury monks. He added that his contact was not directly with ghosts, but depended on tapping into latent historical memories which he termed 'Greater Memory' or 'Memoria', that had echoes of the Theosophists' akashic records and Jung's notions of the collective unconscious. To me that's perfectly reasonable, although I'm completely aware of how wobbly such things can be. He was also a member of the Freemasons, the Theosophical Society, the Society for Psychical Research, the Societas Rosicruciana in Anglia and the Ghost Club. In co-authorship with the Anglican priest Thomas Simcox Lea, he also published the provocatively titled *Gematria: A Preliminary Investigation of the Cabala Contained in the Coptic Gnostic Books.*

How does he fit in with the Templars? Well, I would guess that both Sir Henry and Bligh Bond were Freemasons. In those days, a century ago, anyone who was anyone sought to join the Craft, as they called it. And of course there are Templar degrees within the masonic structures, particularly the York Rite. Masonic influence (in the UK at least), has certainly waned dramatically in this second decade of the 21st Century: the same sort of (often quite dreadful) people now only try their mysterious grips on the handles of their 7-irons, as they seek to get into the best golf clubs instead.

The font dates from about 1300 and is decorated with leaf friezes including Green Men. There is also on the north wall a carved representation of Christ in Majesty seated above a skull. We'll come back to that skull later.

The front porch of the church is crowned with an equi-armed cross, but here you have to excuse my tendency to see what I want to see: Christians who have never heard of Templars or the cross pattée still use them in abundance. But there is also the stained glass window of the Agnus Dei, the Lamb of God, holding the flag of St George, right next to another window depicting St Michael – two of the saints particularly revered by the Templars (the other two being St. Longinus and  St. Mauritius). Some writers have argued that the Agnus Dei within a building is always a sign that the Templars have been involved.

I can't find as to when the stained glass windows were fitted, but they can't have been ancient. I'll guess that Messrs Newbolt and Bond, inspired by their own  masonic neo-Templar mythos, decided to upgrade this odd little church. I'll write to the archivists at the Masonic research lodge in London, known by the splendid name of Quatuor Coronati, and see if they can find out; if there is no connection I won't tell you. And no, I'm not, never have been, and never will be, either a freemason or a golfer.

There is also the very odd locked portal in the north wall known simply as the Priest's Door dated back to 1300 which – to me – sings with Sufi influence. The trefoil window above was added in 1420.

But I really will have to break away from Orchardleigh now. There is a yarn about the people excavating the long barrow there who, on moving aside one of the stones, found an almost bottomless pit beneath. I feel that I'm falling into this, because the more I look the more I uncover. Honestly the beauty of the place becomes painful. Next time I visit, I really must put that armour back on again for my own protection.

You can stay if you want but I'm getting out of here…

Chapter 7

'In the end is my beginning'

Today is April 23rd, St George's Day. This is the patron saint of England, whose flag is a red cross on a white field. Although this symbol has often been appropriated by members of the extreme right in English politics, St George has always been a prophetic figure venerated by Jews, Christians and Muslims. Some of the latter see him as akin to al-Khidr, the 'Green Prophet', who is further syncretised in Armenia with John the Baptist. I like the sound of al-Khidr, but after being sucked into the faery-vortex at Orchardleigh I want to push him aside and get back on track.

I'm a bit grotty today because I had a long dream last night in which Paul McCartney spoke to me. He didn't say anything interesting and his conversation – compared with Prince Harry's – was desultory. It was all I could do not to mention Heather Mills to punish him, or point out that his singing was off-key on the opening of the Olympics. Honestly, if there are higher powers trying to do things for me at liminal levels, they need to show a bit more flair and imagination. Or if my higher mind is trying to find imagery which might help me bridge the gap between normal and supra-normal awareness then it will have to do better than this. Sir Paul was boring.

Having dropped Margaret off at the train station to send her on her way to Gomorrah (my private name for Brussels), I'm now writing this in a little café after having read all their free newspapers. One of the red-tops devotes its front page to the imminent birth of another prince, and half a page near the sport section to the imminent destruction of the world. This is expected today, when the planet Niburu emerges from nowhere and collides with our Earth. This is the time of the Rapture, apparently, and is inescapable because it is so clearly predicted within the Bible, according to some chap from Tennessee.

I'd better get on with this then, and hope they hurry up with the Full English breakfast I've just ordered....

***

So what have we created for this telesmic image so far?

Well, we have the classic Templar form (easy to visualise) and the name of Ancuellos just to pin it in our minds. We have a notional date of 1307 and also the Templar back-story dating from the Order's beginnings. We can place him at the preceptory on the Ridgeway and have him going to the church at Alton Priors. We have even given him a grave in Orchardleigh.

Now it doesn't matter that the grave might well belong to someone else entirely and have nothing whatsoever to do with the Poor Knights. After all, throughout Britain and Europe there are several graves of King Arthur, Merlin, Lancelot, Morgana and the rest, not to mention several world-wide sites for Jesus' grave. (Personally, I just love Ralph Ellis' argument that Jesus died in a Roman prison in the town of Chester. It doesn't matter to me if he is right or not.)

So there is quite a bit to give Ancuellos as much substance as 'Philip'. As we go along on our ride, visiting the Templar sites mentioned earlier, I will be very disappointed if we don't get any manifestations. As long they're not in company with Paul McCartney again.

What about nationality though? Although Google Translate identifies the name as Spanish that doesn't mean a thing. Because a 'name' is important, as I mentioned earlier, a list of Masters within England goes:

- Humbert de Pairaud (1270)
- Gui de Foresta (1275)
- Robert de Torteville (1276)
- Henri de Faverham (1277–1278)
- Robert de Torteville (1280)
- Gui de Foresta (1288)
- Robert de Haleghton (1290–1294 Yorkshire)
- Guillaume de Tourville (1292)
- Gui de Foresta (1293–1296)
- Brian le Jay (1296–1298)
- Guillaume de la More (1298–1307)

The last one, more commonly written up by Franco-phobe Brits as *William de la More* would have been the Master to reckon with at the time of the Order's suppression. If we ever have to 'release' Ancuellos, then he is the figure to use, *a la* General Haig. Oh - and there is also the wonderfully named Amberaldus, described as 'Master of the Templars in England' – possibly in 1229 - although nothing seems to be known about him. He can come through to me any time. If I hadn't already used the name 'Ancuellos' for our telesmic image I'd have seized upon that one.

I've assumed that Ancuellos is from the country we now know as France, perhaps from the deep south and therefore heavily swayed by the Cathars of that region. He was influenced by the Benedictines and also the Cistercian Order of St Bernard which developed from the former. As part of his spiritual life he would acknowledge the Saints Michael, Mauritius, Longinus and George. He would have especial reverence – perhaps without knowing why – for Mary Magdalen. It is quite possible (and we'll look at this later) that the Christ he revered was not that of Jesus, but of John the Baptist.

***

I've just realised that, as I sit here finishing my excellent breakfast and waiting for the Planet Nibiru to come smashing into us, I've assumed too much knowledge in my follow-rider again. We've given Ancuellos a grave, but how did the Order as a whole come to an end? We might as well as sketch that now…

***

The phrase 'In the end is my beginning' came from Mary, Queen of Scots when she knew her execution was imminent. It might as well apply to the Knights Templar also because their sudden and quite spectacular end burned them into the collective mind of the West. Quite simply the Knights Templar were no longer the golden boys of that era. When the Muslims re-took Jerusalem, it shook the very foundation of the Templars. Their whole *raison d'etre* was to protect the Holy Land and keep it pure. More Crusades were launched, in desperation, by Louis IX of France and Edward I of England, but the Templar warriors acting as back-up were increasingly beaten and quickly lost all of their castles in Outremer. After the Siege of Acre in 1291, they were forced to relocate their headquarters to the island of Cyprus.

At this time King Philip IV of France was deeply in debt to the Order. He took advantage of those turbulent times and on Friday the 13th of October, 1307, he ordered the arrest of all the Order's members in France and accused them of all manner of heresies. Many were tortured into giving false confessions, and then burned at the stake.

Although Pope Clement V cleared them of all the charges in 1308, he did not actual publish his findings in what became known as the Chinon Parchment found centuries later when it was *slightly* too late to save anyone. And so on the 18 March 1314, Jacques de Molay the 23rd and last Grand Master of the Order of the Temple, along with his loyal second in command Geoffroi de Charney, were brought before their judges on an island in the Seine. These men, along with most of the other knights, had suffered monstrous torture and long imprisonment at the hands of the Inquisition. They had recanted during the tortures and could have saved their lives now. Instead, de Molay told the judges that indeed he had been guilty, not of the crimes imputed to them, but of basely betraying their Order to save their own lives. It was pure and holy; the charges were fictitious and the confessions false.

So they were burned at the stake, but before the flames took his voice Jacques de Molay cursed the Pope and said that within a year and a day both he and Philip IV would be obliged to answer for their crimes in God's presence. In the event Philip and Clement V both died within a year of the execution: Clement succumbing to a long illness on 20 April 1314, and Philip dying due to a stroke while hunting. In fact King Philip's whole line perished, and within fourteen years of the death of Molay, the 300-year-old House of Capet collapsed.

So it began.

I'd follow a man like Jacques de Molay

***

Well I'm home now and waiting for Margaret to Skype me from Gomorrah. There are still a few hours of daylight left but no sign of the Planet Niburu. I think I might be okay. Tomorrow I plan to catch the train to Bristol, taking my own sandwiches with me, and spend some time strolling around the ruined Temple Church there. Then, when I've had a good brood, I'll outline the accusations made against them, some of which are quite ridiculous. Then again, if I'd been a humble knight, being inflicted by the sort of tortures that only the disgusting and unholy Holy Inquisition could devise, I would have confessed to anything, agreed to any heresy or perversion, betrayed any of my colleagues, just to get them to stop. That's why I have no sympathy for Mary, Queen of Scots because she would have brought England and Scotland back under the yoke of Rome, where the members of the Inquisition were regarded as the good guys. We would never had the Reformation or the sublime Enlightenment - otherwise known as the Age of Reason.

***

I'm worried about that chap from Tennessee. Like Carl Jung's ghosts he was expecting something amazing – in his case the Rapture, an End Time event when all Christian believers - living and dead - will rise into the sky and join their Christ. Maybe something of that sort happened back in Tennessee, but the skies above Wiltshire today are clear and pure and we do have a new Prince of the Realm: Prince Louis Arthur Charles. Heirs to the throne in this country are invariably given the name Arthur along with the others. Just in case one of them is the Once and Future King. Conspiracy Theorists have long argued that Charles had to marry Diana in order to access the Spencer bloodline which is, they say, rather sacred. I'm not a great fan of sacred bloodlines but I do think Princes William and Harry are thoroughly decent fellas, and all thanks to their mum.

Mind you I did have a rotten night's sleep and woke up several times just to make notes of things I must add to this manuscript in due course. No revelations from higher sources, just simple things I must point out with respect to the Avebury complex. By the time you read this, they will already have been placed. Because Margaret is away, and I'm now retired, I can do this quite happily. But I did have a brief dream about being part of some medieval field hospital – the sort that would have been attached to an army. It was a bit of a joke dream, really, because there were no patients and the equipment was entirely modern; my dream-self was having a bit of a laugh.

Anyway, now that I've survived the Planet Nibiru and the Rapture and am about to catch the train to Bristol, I'm determined to view every event of my mini-pilgrimage as a secret dealing between myself and, well, all sorts of Things that are bubbling up within me, like those turbulences at the Broad Well. Do feel free to sit next to me on the train this time. Just don't talk: at barbers and on public transport I don't like conversation.

***

Ten hours after writing that last I can look back upon a fruitful day. I won't go into *all* the details, simply because I get bored by the sound of my own voice. But I did take my little pie-bald stone with me, holding it my left hand

and so soaking up impressions and sights from my right brain as we sped through the delightful scenery from Bradford on Avon to Bath, and then on toward Bristol. The only other way I could have shown it this new realm would have been by holding it up to the glass and talking to it, but that might have got me arrested.

I'm not being entirely silly here. I really do believe that *everything* – no matter how small and apparently inanimate – has its own level of consciousness. If there were a fire in our house, for example, the two 'live-wood' wands that were given to me by Dusty Miller would be rescued before anything else. I'll see in time whether my little templar stone with its as-yet secret name might get empowered to the same formidable extent as these.

Of course, as I set out, it poured with rain. Actually it hail-stoned. *Come on lads, give me a break!* I implored to whatever members of the Order might have been overseeing this. By the time I got to Bristol it was perfect walking weather.

On the map the Temple Church was only a short distance from Temple Meads train station. As ever, I got completely lost, as invariably happens when Margaret is not around. I seemed to be wandering endlessly around high-rise apartment blocks and getting agitated. It was only when I saw through trees the flutter of a distant flag – the Cross of St George – and headed toward it, that I found myself next to a pub called The Ship, and was able to get my bearings.

The Temple Church itself was bombed to buggery during Second World War. Both Bristol and Bath suffered badly. Only its framework remains, although it's famously tilted tower still tilts. This relatively modern construction (1460) was built on the site of a previous, round church of the first Knights Templar in this area which was built in 1145, on land granted to them by Robert of Gloucester. This was also known as the Holy Cross Church. He also gave them the surrounding land on which to build a Priory for themselves. It wasn't particularly good land being very marshy, but at that time most of the land outside the city walls was like that. This is still echoed in some of district and street names of modern Bristol, such as Canon's Marsh and Marsh Street. The eastern part of the marshland was known as Temple Fee but I've been unable to find an origin for 'Fee'. While I'd love to think it was derived from fay, or fae or faery it is most probably a variant of *feudum*, from the Frankish *fehu,* and referred to the place where they kept their cattle.

They occupied this land for the better part of the next 200 years but when they were suppressed the English king at the time, Edward II, reluctantly had the Templars in Bristol arrested and thrown in the castle dungeons, where most were killed - although the Knights of Saint John, a sister Order, did manage to rescue a few.

It was they who took over the Templars land, demolished the old Temple and built a much finer one, Temple Church, but still retained the original circular (some say oval) holy space within their far larger edifice.

On my Big Day Out I had planned to stroll around within the surviving, roofless, column-less round nave that once had an aisle arcade, and a chancel with a semi-circular apse. I would do some hard-core but exceedingly silent invocation if there was no-one around. As it was, the whole building is now sealed off and described as Unsafe to Enter. I had to take that as a metaphor for this particular journey. Peering through the railings I could see the round area which most attracted me. I poked my phone through and took a photo but the fierce sun was right into the lens and the only thing I could capture was an amber splodge. That was a metaphor too.

Interestingly, I did learn later about the famous exorcism of George Lukins in 1788, who had exhibited all the signs of demonic possession that are familiar to us today from numerous movies. Previously of good and stable character in his Bristol parish, he suddenly believed that he *was* the Devil, made barking noises, spoke in tongues, sang an inverted *Te Deum* and was extremely violent. For a time they moved him from Bristol and incarcerated him in St George's Hospital in Tooting, in a ward for the Insane. In his more lucid moments he declared that he had become possessed by seven demons, who could only be driven out by seven clergymen from different denominations. Eventually he was taken back to Bristol again to the Temple Church where seven terrified clergymen, mainly Methodist and Anglican, used the Trinitarian formula to banish all his demons. This caused great controversy at the time, and a certain Dr. Feriar, a 'medical demonologist', criticised George Lukins as an impostor masquerading as a demoniac. That may be, but after the exorcism Lukins was described as calm and happy and seems to have lived so for the rest of his life.

For me, the significance of this very true and well-documented story is that the respectable clergymen of varied denominations should have recognised Temple Church as a place of sufficient power and sanctity as to support their joint effort.

Did this skeleton of a church radiate Templar energies? Did it send my nape hairs prickling? Did I get *anything* from the place?

Not a thing.

***

I was pretty tired by this time so I made my way to Arnolfini's. I used to go there a lot in the early 70's in my sub-hippy days, when it was a rough and ready but still enormously appealing arty-farty café on the other side of the river. Now it claims to be one of Europe's leading centres for the contemporary arts.

I ordered a bacon sandwich from a surly, mustachioed young man behind the counter and it was all he could do just to make conversation, although he took my money fast enough. But then - marvelous to see – a gorgeous young woman with purple and silver streaks in her hair came up and placed her order and he couldn't have been more attentive toward her, or more articulate.

Of course, in my new frame of thinking that day I knew that this wasn't a case of a young man being irritated by an old git and then having his hormones excited by this young and exotic totty. No no no... He must have been a Templar in a previous life and had now come to Bristol where, as with Jung's revenants, he 'found not what he had sought'. Yet, to his delight, he was now being enchanted by an actual *peri.* Now in Islam the *peris* are beautiful female spirits who often appear to humans to tempt, punish or even abduct, and can appear physically or even spiritually. This young creature from Outremer was stunning.

The two of them disappeared around the back.

The bacon butty, when it came, was somewhat burnt but still excellent.

***

It was when I got the train back that I had the most pertinent encounter, still clutching my little stone. There was hardly anyone on board but I felt an impulse to

103

change my seat so as to face direction of travel. The train stopped at Bath and an overweight, middle aged woman with lank grey hair sat opposite me. She was wearing an old, shapeless, knitted sweater with the faded pattern of an eight-petalled flower on the front. As she plonked her Dr. Martens handbag on the little table between us I noticed that it was adorned with a glorious mirror-image of St George killing his dragon and waving his flag.

Here's what I **didn't** say:

I'm writing about St George at the moment. Do you know anything about the Templars?

I didn't say anything because she didn't know I existed. She didn't know that she was on a train or even that the world around her was still turning and churning. She was waving to a man on the platform as the train pulled away and I've never seen anyone so happy, so ecstatic. It was as if she had raised within herself some arcane Serpent Power because light was shooting out of her face and through the flower on her tatty sweater. Her whole being was exploding with bliss and I knew that at that moment, the dumpy little woman with the tacky bag, was one of the Shining Ones. As the train pulled away she sank back in her seat, closed her eyes and she was in rapture, as her world had begun and not ended. She had come to Bath, and found that which she had sought.

I looked at the image of St George battling away with his dragon and knew that whatever the real secret behind the Templars was, whatever the nature of their fabled treasure, nothing could compare with the wealth that woman had found just then.

Chapter 8

Sins and their Echoes.

It is raining heavily today, so although Margaret is back we won't be going on any more Templar jaunts and picnics just yet. We'll have to travel inwardly instead, which often covers harder ground. (Does that sound a bit pompous?)

On a bleak day like today, what exactly were the Templar crimes? Or rather, what were they *accused* of doing that King Philip was able to use against them? You see the thing is, if we're going to create this telesmic image known as Ancuellos, we don't want to imbed something dreadful into his rather hazy consciousness – which at the moment is entirely *our* consciousness.

Here are the main ones…

1. Entrants to the Order had to deny Christ, the Virgin Mary and the saints
2. They were told that Christ was a false prophet and there was no hope of salvation through him
3. They rejected the sacraments of the Catholic church
4. Knights were ordered to spit on a crucifix or urinate or trample on it
5. This idol was encircled with cords, which the Templars then wore around their waists
6. The Grand Master and other leading Templars could absolve sins even though they were laymen and not priests

7. New entrants were kissed on the mouth, the navel, the stomach, the buttocks and the spine and buggery was encouraged
8. The Templars were only interested in financial gain and pocketed donations for their own use.
9. They worshipped a head of some description, or an idol called Baphomet

I can't see much wrong with any of them.

Nos. **1, 2** and **3** are already part and parcel of my psyche, as much as anything is these days.

I wouldn't personally, as in no. **4**, spit, urinate or trample on a cross or a crescent or an ankh or even a shirt from Sunderland Football Club. In any case their argument to the Inquisitors was that they were preparing new Knights for the things they would be made to do if they ever got caught by the Saracen. It's rather like the modern Special Forces today, who undergo tortures in training to ready them for the real thing.

No. **5** – cords? Don't they do they do similar with cords in the money-making Kabbalah movement today? (I've written several books on the Kabbalibosh and have never once used or sold – oh give me strength! - Kabbalah Water or Red Cords.)

As for no. **6** I have always wrestled with self-forgiveness of my own stupidities. The older I get the more I flog myself, though without becoming one of the flagellating idiots in Opus Dei wo are so influential in the European Commission and its octopus-like tentacles today. Margaret says I should become my own Templar Master and absolve myself.

No. **7**? I wouldn't particularly want to be slobbered over and buggered, but I can't for the life of me take offence at any man or woman who enjoyed that.

Jacques de Molay himself, at his trial, admitted that he *had* defamed the cross but had *not* indulged in homosexuality. If he had simply reversed his statement he probably would have been released. I think it was the Benedictine Order which sanctioned what was once known as interfemoral intercourse, which was a non-penetrative sex, in which a male places his penis between a brother monk's thighs, and thrusts to create friction and achieve orgasm. And in the light of the massive paedophilia scandals which have hit all Christian denominations in the late 20th and early 21st Centuries, mutual buggery was hardly explosive news even in the early 14th Century.

No. **8**, the financial gain. I think this happens to any Order or spiritual organisation when it gets too big. I'm still not convinced that it didn't become a Ponzi scheme in its last years.

And crucially no. **9**, the worship of a head they called Baphomet. I'll talk about this later when we've visited the place on the Ridgeway known as Templar Bottom, and an otherwise un-remarked on area called Man's Head.

***

But as I sit here pen in hand looking over these, all of which I'll come back to in due course, it's No. 6, the Templars' absolution of sin without needing the malign intermediaries within the Holy Church to do so. That keeps waving to me.

One of the torments in my own life is a sense of guilt at all the stupid things I've done. In one job I had I was suspended from work and ultimately given a final formal warning, because instead of going to my lipreading class I went home instead, on a gloriously sunny afternoon. Hardly a monstrous crime, you'll probably agree, but at the time I felt the world of the work-place looked at me with disgust. Actually, they couldn't give a toss, and the auto-da-fé which followed was more to do with the internal politics of my inept managers. Yet for such an inconsequential, victimless crime, I felt hugely guilty.

Which brings me back to the Templars at the time of their arrest. Do those who have reincarnated have this sort of thing hanging over them? Do they have some wicked barb of guilt buried deep within? Most of them probably never got anywhere near what we imagine were the Inner Mysteries. They would have been the Useful Idiots of their time and place. Did they, in their cells awaiting torture and execution, start to think as I thought then – but magnified a million times? When they went to the stake did they think of themselves as fallen men, objects of disgust?

Maybe that was more truly the nature of the demons that possessed George Lukins: an unconscious and overwhelming of guilt from a previous Templar life which made him suddenly feel that he had, somewhere at some time and in the eyes of the world, broken all the spiritual laws, and so had to be exorcised at the actual Templar Church in his home town.

And as I write this that wonderfully powerful name Amberaldus also comes in, pushing all other things out.

Bear with me…

- Amber is a fossilised resin from extinct trees. It was once enormously popular because of its strange properties that my rider can look up later, not least the fact that some items had insects, seeds, flowers trapped within its golden glow that had existed a million years ago. Amber also means 'fierce' in Gaelic.

- Aldus is a name of Old German origin, meaning 'Old One'.

I feel that in some way Ancuellos is shaping up to be an avatar of this mysterious Fierce Old One Amberaldus, as Krishna was an avatar of Vishnu. At some time, in some appropriate place on this ride across Templar levels of Wiltshire, I might try and use the powerful image of Amberaldus to call out to the far memories of all those sucked into the Order's vortex: *Listen lads – you did nothing wrong! Jacques de Molay said it himself: You are, and always were, as Pure and Holy as anyone. Pax Vobiscum to you all.*

If I were to do this would it have any effect whatsoever? I don't know. Yet lone individuals incessantly pray for peace at times of world torment and disaster without worrying about the effectiveness of the spiritual mechanics involved. If, as I suspect, there is no such thing as linear time, and we are all inter-connected at the deepest levels, then it will be worth a try. At very least it will clear my own mind of any notions that they were 'mad, bad and dangerous to know' as Lady Lamb once said of Lord Byron. Then when we do activate Ancuellos he will be a good 'un.

***

Phew… that came out of the blue. Perhaps because it is April 30th today, when Moorish troops landed at Gibraltar to begin their conquest of the Iberian Peninsula, George

Washington was inaugurated as first President of the U.S.A., Hitler and Eva Braun committed suicide, Iran nationalised its oil fields, South Vietnam surrendered, Chrysler filed for bankruptcy and the Deepwater Horizon oil reached the American coast. Of course, I knew that about Hitler but got the rest from Wikipedia. And this was the date when *Riverdance* was first performed in the interval of the Eurovision Song Contest in 1994. I make no apologies for that addition. It is also, this evening, the Feast of St Walpurga, the night when, in Germanic lore, witches dance to the Devil, when graves are opened and the dead come forth. I'll take my templarised stone to bed, under the pillow and see what happens…

***

And now today is May 1st! I wish I could boast of powerful dreams last night involving wild witches adoring me as their Master on the Harz Mountains, but I only had distorted (very happy) versions of the annual 'Paper 'Plane Contest' I used to organise at the now defunct Ashton Street Centre: prizes for longest flight, best design, most aerobatic, most bizarre. My core group won every time and it's completely untrue that I doctored the score board.

But I can put such silliness aside and rescue the stone from under the pillow because today is Beltain. The name originates from the Celtic god Bel meaning 'the bright one' and the Gaelic word 'teine' meaning fire. Some have argued that Tan Hill, which is almost opposite the Templar Door, was originally *Teine* Hill, a reference to the fire festivals they would once have had there – and indeed still had until late Victorian times. Terence Meaden argues that the annual May Fertility Festival is the time of the consummation of the gods between Sun and Earth, and feels that the Neolithic Earth Goddess for the Avebury people was Tara and the Sky Father Taran.

Would Ancuellos have been aware of May Day as he stood within the doorframe at Alton Priors? After all, there is a Green Man on the font of his Orchardleigh Church. There would certainly have been local rites and traditions that he might have cast a leery or even jealous eye upon. But May Day has always had an undercurrent that is nicely summed up by the writers of the web-site *The Goddess and the Green Man*:

> On May Eve the sexuality of life and the earth is at its peak. Abundant fertility, on all levels, is the central theme. The Maiden goddess has reached her fullness. She is the manifestation of growth and renewal, Flora, the Goddess of Spring, the May Queen, the May Bride. The Young Oak King, as Jack-In-The-Green, as the Green Man, falls in love with her and wins her hand. The union is consummated and the May Queen becomes pregnant. Together the May Queen and the May King are symbols of the Sacred Marriage (or Heiros Gamos), the union of Earth and Sky, and this union has merrily been re-enacted by humans throughout the centuries.

I suppose that even as I ponder this I'm still projecting my own Earth Magicky concerns onto and into this convenient eidolon. If our man had any historical reality then I feel sure he would have been wondering how he could get out of the Order entirely, but agonising as to where he could go. It seems that each knight had to serve three campaigns on land and two on the sea before they were allowed home, which seems a bit of a rip-off to me.

By the time they did get back many of them were either sick or wounded and effectively penniless. It was then up to the loyalty of those Knights who stayed at home to provide them with land.

Remember that for them, in their time, it was not simply a question of finding themselves a job as ordinary folk today like ourselves would do. They needed land – which for them would be synonymous with money and security. In 1307, just as today, the ordinary folk would have taken a secret pleasure in the Templars' downfall and mutter the old one about 'How are the Mighty fallen…' One SAS man I knew observed that within the Regiment he was a fighting cock; on Civvy Street, he was just a feather duster. Outside the security of the Order the Templars walked the fine line between being disgraced and feeling disgraceful.

What I learn from all this, is that the closer I ride toward the inner Templar heartlands, the nearer I get to their Mysteries, I still don't feel awe, or trembling. I actually feel enormously sorry for them, and I don't care if they think that patronising and pisses them off

Poor old buggers… is all I can say at the moment.

Chapter 9

The White World

Not sure what date it is today but the weather is glorious. I'm scribbling this in Trowbridge Library waiting for Margaret to meet me after her gym session. And I'm excited because we'll shoot out straight away for a picnic. This excites me because a) I like picnics and b) we're going to Temple Bottom and the Glory Ann ponds.

Until yesterday I began to think that the Templars didn't like me. Things kept going wrong, data kept getting lost, whole books disappeared, inflammations of my throat and ears and sinuses which Margaret refers to as my 'Templar Head', blaming them entirely. A strange, perhaps inconsequential thing happened yesterday that made me think *hmmmm....do they trust me now?*

Years ago, 1998-ish, I got out of the library in Bradford on Avon a small book about walks across Wiltshire. In that was the very first mention of the Templar sites just off the Ridgeway, a photo of the so-called 'Templar bath', and the nearby Glory Ann ponds. Since then, unusually for me, I completely forgot the book's title and author, but those names stuck in my mind.

Recently, googling every possible reference to the Glory Ann ponds in particular, I could find virtually nothing. I scoured the local sections in Bradford on Avon, Trowbridge and Melksham libraries, and used various searches: *Wiltshire Walks, Wiltshire Trails, Wiltshire Folklore* etc, but still couldn't find the book. Then yesterday, just as I had finished typing up bits and pieces in Trowbridge's excellent library, I swivelled in my chair to leave when, displayed openly on the shelf where it hadn't been the day before, was *Exploring Historic Wiltshire (Volume 1: North)* by Ken Watts. Within that, complete with Ordnance Survey references, were all the details I needed to make an accurate visit to the site of their preceptory – and find the supine megalith known locally (VERY locally, as no-one else on-line has ever heard of it) as the 'Templar bath'.

I decided to make my pilgrimage special. This morning I had my hair cut by my favourite Moroccan barber (Monday-Thursday. Seniors £6.50). I asked him to do it short, a No. 2 cut so that I would look hard and vaguely menacing. Then I went home and showered, put on clean socks and clean underpants. Alas the latter were not, like the Templar requirement, made of wool, just honest free-range cotton, nothing pervy. Then I put on my clean walking clothes (cargo trousers and shirt with *lots* of pockets), cleaned my boots, got a clean handkerchief - which one of my daughters had turned into a mouse (a skill I once had but have long since lost) – and was ready

I thought I'd make an effort.

Then along with map, Ken Watts' book, several pairs of reading glasses in case the ones I get from the Poundland break on my unusually large (in more than one way) head, my templarish stone in my heart pocket, and our wands, I was ready.

***

But as I write this I've just remembered one of my dreams last night. I spent some time talking to the actor Mark Ryan, who in reality in 1994-ish, got me drunk on two half-shandies one night in a Bathford pub. I first became aware of Mark in the long-running telly series *Robin of Sherwood*, in which he was the Islamic character Nasir, the one with two swords. A deeply psychic man, with something of a covert military background which ran alongside his impressive acting career, he was very amicable in my dream. I've realised, too, that when I meet these liminal figures I am always very shy and don't have much to offer. Still, given Mark Ryan's style, I think 'he' is a little closer to what I need in order to step up with my Higher Self toward or into the Templar egregore.

Anyway… off we go!

***

That was all yesterday, and I must say what a splendid outing we had…

We drove past Avebury and took the road up to and slightly beyond the White Horse of Hackpen Hill, to

the small car park on the Great Ridgeway. I should explain that these hill carvings, as I think I've described them, aren't chiselled out like the heads on Mount Rushmore. The hills of Wiltshire are known, perhaps confusingly, as areas of chalk downland. The term 'downs' derives from an old Celtic word for hills. If you were to cut away the turf you would expose the tough white chalk underneath. Which is how the Victorian farmer created the horse at Alton Barnes, and how the ancients created the Cerne Abbas ithyphallic giant and the dragon-like White Horse of Uffington.

Soldiers in both wars carved their regimental badges on the hillsides above their camps, which are still regularly scoured clean. The Hackpen Horse is a spindly little thing you can't help but like. It is also on the hill which has various tales of faery enchantment that I won't go into here lest I get sucked in again.

It is hard to give an idea as to how ancient this area is. Palaeolithic flints were recovered by a certain Mr. Kendall in 1912 during excavations on this hill, so people have been living and loving and fighting and surviving and trading and dreaming in this area for tens upon tens of thousands of years.

Our first stop was the Glory Ann ponds, perhaps two miles along in a straight line. As ever I got us lost; as ever Margaret put me right. (She does a wicked impersonation of me being pixie-led.) Until Ken Watts' tome magickally appeared I could find almost no information about the Glory Ann pond except for two lines in one book about the sinister atmosphere in that immediate area. It is, apparently, a place of suicides, murders and muggings. There is almost nothing on-line except a brief reference on a local archaeological website which said: 'To the east of Monkton Down is an area known as Templar Bottom, where the Knights Templar had a preceptory in the 12th and 13th centuries, just east of Glory Ann Pond.'

The deliciously wacky and sometimes inspired William Stukeley visited in 1724 and later wrote about this immediate location in his book *Abury – a Temple of the British Druids*. He described in detail the monstrous long barrow and complex of megaliths that he called the Old Chapel, which he felt was the tomb of an Archdruid and also a mortuary enclosure. No trace remains of the

Old Chapel today, which is quite heart-breaking. Ken Watts mentioned a brooding atmosphere to this whole area that local walkers have attributed to the ghosts of the Templars. But he, like myself now, think it more likely to do with ancestors buried within the Old Chapel four thousand years ago who haven't quite forgiven our destructions since Stukeley's visit.

The latter also wrote about a 'singular excavation' next to it, a 'pyriform concavity, set with stones on the inside' and known locally as the Balmore pond, which was supposed by the locals to have a secret vault beneath it. He speculated that the pond was a place of executions. I can find no other reference to this Balmore pond. This *must* be another name for the Glory Ann, as it is set in the same precise location.

There are actually two ponds though the smaller one is, apparently, sometimes dried up. The larger of the ponds, the Glory Ann itself, is described as a clay pit, or elsewhere as a 'brickpit'. I don't know what either of these terms mean. I don't know whether it (somehow) has a natural source of water or whether it was once filled artificially. If the latter, the water has never drained or evaporated over the centuries. In 1820 it was described on

117

local maps as Glory Ann or Port Lorien. Ken Watts (may his name be blest) wrote that both Parish Registers and Census returns in the 19th Century sometimes nominate 'L'Orient' as the alternative name for Glory Ann, and feels that this was a local nod to the Templars' time in the Middle East when the Far East was unknown. He also opined that Glory Ann was a corruption from the Templar motto:

'**Non nobis Domine**, **non nobis**, **sed nomini tuo da gloriam**.'

Meaning in English, 'Not to us Lord, not to us, but to Your Name give the glory.' I am certain this is where the name came from, so regardless of whether these 'clay pits' existed in the 13th and 14th Centuries, they are somehow linked with the Templars, whose preceptory off the Ridgeway was within spitting distance.

Several times when I have been within the aura – real or imagined – of Templar sites, I have quietly intoned this motto. I can't say that anything happened, but I felt it was akin to using a password to gain access. Margaret and I, in old churches, have a copy of the Paternoster that we will quietly intone, with the idea that the Old Language (Latin!) will wake them up. Sometimes it does.

Again, I can't pretend that anything cosmic happened here except for a feeling of gladness that we had found the place. I had brought me with me the name of the only known Templars in Wiltshire after the Order was suppressed in England in 1308: John de Mohun, John de Egle, Robert de Hameldon, and Robert de Sautré, I don't know what happened to them but I felt that by uttering their names over the face of the waters of the Glory Ann pond it might do them some good.

And I did pause next to the great flat field which had once been the site of Stukeley's 'Old Chapel' and apologised to all those forgotten souls whose bits and pieces had been interred, and whose megalithic sepulchre had been ripped apart and ultimately flattened by the modern world. The Order of the Poor Knights had left them well alone during their time on these heights; they were crushed by Victorian farmers who ploughed their fields and scattered their good seeds on the land.

***

Then the walk down the (un-signposted) path to Temple Bottom and Temple Farm was painless and exceedingly pleasant.

I thought that I would visualise myself in the 'god-form' of a Templar Master, Amberaldus himself, and make rather a splendid entrance, at some level, into their former lands that had been established by John Mareschall in 1155. I must have looked like a great ship in full sail; good job there was no-one about. Yet nothing happened at any level that I was aware of.

I think that the Templars here might have been quite happy. After all they were in the enviable position of being exempt from taxes, exempt from the scrutiny of the Church, and many of their workers and tenants also enjoyed this privilege. They might have enjoyed life on the Ridgeway and in this valley, even if their primary role, now that the Holy Land had fallen forever, was to breed sheep. Ken Watts again, found a reference to sheep husbandry at Temple Rockley where it is recorded that they milked sheep to make cheese, and added that a Knight once expressed outrage at being posted to England by exclaiming: 'We are preceptors of sheep!'

But by Ancuellos' time sheep was where the money lay, as wool became the backbone and driving force of the medieval English economy between the late thirteenth century and late fifteenth century. No form of manufacturing had a greater impact upon the economy and society of Ancuellos' time than did those industries producing cloths from various kinds of wool. The trade was described as 'the jewel in the realm' and to this day under the seat of the Lord High Chancellor in the House of Lords is a large square bag of wool called the 'woolsack', a reminder of the principal source of English wealth in the Middle Ages. You cannot over-estimate the demand for it. Everyone who had land, from peasants to major landowners, raised sheep. At that time the best weavers lived in Flanders and in the rich cloth-making towns of Bruges, Ghent and Ypres, they were ready to pay top prices for English wool.

The Templars' *Agnus Dei* – the Lamb of God – would have taken on a slightly different significance by this time.

***

Well, we didn't have any cosmic explosions of insight again, nor yet were assailed by Templar revenants wanting succour. But at least we did find the Templar

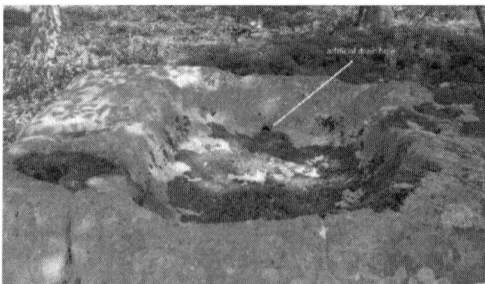 bath. I challenge you to find anything about that on-line. Yet it is a massive megalith, 15' by 11', hollowed out and with a

drain hole in one side. No-one really knows what it was used for. It could have been for baptism, or perhaps draining blood from small animals. It wasn't deep enough for any adult to stretch out, but a Knight could have washed his bollocks in it, and that might have been a real delight in those days.

We didn't linger because it seemed to be on private land and we both had a fear of 'slavering dogs' being set upon us although that was highly unlikely. There was a scattering of houses in this supremely quiet valley but not a glimpse of anyone.

I won't try and spin out our winding walk back to the car park because it would read too much like one of the 'path-workings' that sometimes blight the modern mystical world and are really the product of thwarted short-story writers. I will add that our excellent Ordnance Survey map bore little resemblance to the pattern of paths on our return route, and Margaret agrees. I think the cartographers got so entranced by the bucolic atmosphere of this lost realm that they must have said: *Look, this path obviously twists and turns all over the place but let's just draw it as a straight line and go off to the pub. No-one is ever likely to walk here...*

Suffice to say that we saw:

- 2 pure white stallions who came to their fence and let me stroke them.
- 7 pure white horned bullocks.
- 2 circling hobbies, which Templars would have used as birds of prey for hawking.
- 2 magnificent trees in a vast ploughed field which the farmer had obviously left alone, rather than dynamiting them. We both agree that the larger

right-hand tree was the Queen, and the smaller companion the King of all the trees in this area.
- 1 sign, in the middle of nowhere, which warned of Toads crossing the path.

We had our flask of tea here and Margaret said she could hear them, doing whatever it is that toads do. It's a bit of a risible signpost, perhaps, as no cars could access this narrow chalk path. But toads themselves are enormously powerful and I dare say liminal creatures. You might trying googling Toad symbolism. I didn't want to sink back into the heavy-duty Ogdoad of Ancient Egypt which obsessed me once, so I clicked on 'toad symbolism' and immediately hit upon Ted Andrews, who urged on Facebook that the creature represents:

> 'Yin and Yang, life and death, good and evil, light and dark... The toad is also considered an astral traveller because he can survive in both worlds - aquatic and the physical. He can be in the spiritual or emotional level represented by water and the physical plane represented by the ground. He is grounded in his spiritual being. While the toad may be a stubborn guide, he often will help you with encouragement. His attention to detail will help in learning to communicate with the spirit world.'

Nothing of occult significance entered my dreams that night but my wife had trouble sleeping. She felt it was something to do with the Templar energies and our walking through what we both agreed was a 'White World'. In fact because of the purity of the air, the silence, the complete lack of people and the feeling of the white chalk beneath the soil, that's exactly what it is seemed like. (Incidentally, she is not enamoured of the Order and blames their obsession with severed heads for the problems I mentioned earlier with my ear/nose/throat/neck/sinuses.)

Later, when I look at the Beausant and also Cathar beliefs to do with Light and Darkness, I'll come back to this.

Chapter 10

Holy Hiatus

'Sod the Templars' said Margaret last night. 'Let's go to the Rollrights tomorrow.'

I was more than happy to agree. Inner work, no matter how exalted or exciting, can just become tedious and draining. Sometimes you must tell the inner things to go away. Just because they – whatever they are – seem to live on a higher level to us doesn't make them infallible. Very often they haven't a clue about what life is like in the material world. That must be even truer of the Templar revenants who poke their heads around in the 21st Century.

Besides, I'd always wanted to visit the Rollright stone circle about 60 miles north of us. William G. Gray, who was something of a teacher to me, even wrote a small book called *The Rollright Ritual*, based upon his experience at the circle when he cycled over there from Cheltenham on a full moon night probably around 1970. I thought I'd take that little tome with me and remember the old sod while Margaret did her own stuff at the circle and inside her lovely head, working at levels I won't easily achieve in this lifetime. It was Bill who used the term 'holy hiatus' to describe those moments in rituals when, amid the silence, between the wavings and weavings of Light, the silent gnosis can arise. Or in other words, I just needed a bit of a rest from all the galloping.

But I must mention quickly just one small dream-sequence I had last night…

I was invited to a wedding. Not *the* wedding which is still coming up, but the entire tone of the dream was that it was uber-posh. I don't know who the bride and groom were and I never even saw them, but the ceremony took place in Bath Abbey with the reception at the Royal Crescent Hotel. (When I lived next to the latter I saw Princess Margaret emerge one morning with a fag in the corner of her mouth and looking as if she'd had a *very* wild night!) So the dream shaped up as being not *quite* royal, yet, but in that direction. Although my wife Margaret was in the dream she wasn't invited and stood on the side-lines. She was despairing that although I wore a 'posh' (that word again!) Armani suit, posh shirt and tie and looked infernally handsome, I spoiled it all by wearing a pair of tawny old moccasins. I was accompanied throughout by a fella called Lesley Kneeling who almost clung to my back. I don't think he was trying to bugger me. Could I have picked up a psychic attachment during all this work? When I see Dee Banton I'll get her to sort this.

I think my subconscious was still trying to boost me up toward the levels of the *hieros gamos* which everyone should aspire toward, and which Picknett and Prince felt might have been an integral part of the Mysteries. Then the whole thing segued into a story in which Margaret tried to get admission to an un-named secret society, yet to do so she had to change her name to Nobby.

(Incidentally it was only a couple of days ago that I stumbled on the scrap of paper I had brought with me from Dee's, well over a year ago. She had 'seen' an unusual symbol on my brow and drew it out for me:
I had no idea what it meant, and nor did she.)

The trip to the Rollrights was easy. I have always thought, over many years, that the sublime and royal county of Gloucestershire didn't like me. This was probably because I had such a dismal time in Gloucester itself in 1974. Visits since always had various niggles attached and I'd never felt entirely comfortable. Mind you I feel the same in Marlborough, in Wiltshire: I don't like the place and it doesn't like me. And unless you've got hours to spare don't get me started on Brussels. But today…today was more than easy, it was guh-lorious.

We set off early enough to avoid the Bank Holiday traffic, were able to park in the small lay-by next to stones and found a group of revellers who had clearly camped within the circle overnight.

Hekas, Hekas, Este Bebeloi! I said to them in my mind, which means 'Be ye far from us o ye profane', and blasted them with my wand. They sort of slunk away, not making eye contact.

But hold on… Did I *really* manage to dismiss them like that? No, of course not. It makes for a great yarn but the fact is they were already packing up to go and they left the circle in a pristine state. I don't really begrudge them being there – and what a night it must have been for them beneath the stars!

But I *did* hope they'd go, and I *was* holding the wand.

***

During this hiatus I can tell you a bit about these wands that I've already brought into my yarns.

I have two 'live-wood' wands called Raven and Crow. These were purely arbitrary names that quickly stuck. They were given to me by Dusty Miller. When I did my first public talk about Dion Fortune at some London university, it was on the understanding that I be given one of these as payment. In the event, he gave me two, and said that the larger one – Raven – had actually been waiting for me.

After the lecture, in the car on the way home, the delight I felt was not because I'd been a shameless poseur before a large crowd, but for the tangible presence of these two wands. The smaller one is about the size and shape of a pencil; the larger, rather the size and shape of an Egyptian *uas* wand. You can look that up yourself. No, they don't want their photos taken, or anything in the way of selfies.

Dusty, I would explain, is a one-off. He is totally, adorably different and probably not entirely human. He can commune with the tree spirits that he calls dryads. Some of them, yearning for movement, are happy to be coaxed willingly into his wands.

'Just act 'as if'', he told me. 'Pretend to believe, suspend disbelief – whatever works for you.'

When I got back to Murhill I wheeled my tiny daughter Zoe around in her pushchair, showing Crow exactly where we lived, in a valley that in itself was never quite within this world. when I slipped him back into my shirt pocket there was an almost audible and disappointed sense of *OH!* from within. I whipped him out and stared hard. *We're going to be such good friends,* I said.

Crow stays within our car. Raven lives in the house but is taken out on our trips. If I want to draw a magickal circle around myself or place of working, I use him. Once or twice I've felt assailed by crude bits and bobs on astral levels and Raven's laser-like tip blasts them. Incidentally it was Paddy who told me that instead of using the old-fashioned Banishing and Invoking patterns of the Pentagram, she always used an outward or inward turning spiral to get the same effect.

When Margaret re-appeared in my life in 2004 she 'got' them immediately. Someday we might write a small book about... well, I was going to say their 'powers', but that is not the right word. Their 'possibilities'? Certainly, they have proved times without number their ability to enhance our own needs and requests in ways that we've both exclaimed: *Wow – thank you lads!*

***

Although this trip to the Rollrights was integral to Margaret's very separate inner work, I had a chance to thank the shades Bill and Bobbie Gray for the profound impact they had upon my life and my magickal upbringing. (I can hear him now saying: 'Without the 'k' please!' but in other contexts I prefer it.) Skimming through his book and underlining things I'd never noticed before I was struck by the fact that the stones of the Kingsmen imparted nothing in the way of philosophising, no occult secrets: just the mundane and everyday bits and pieces of their builders' lives. That to me, at my age, I see as far more important. I get sick of philosophers and their philosophies: they're all the same. They all sound like Mark Edsel's 'Masters' in that book I mentioned earlier. So what was Bill's technique for communing with these stones? Did he summon, stir and call up the spirits with Words of Power and mighty invocations? Did he go into a shamanic trance? No, he used a far simpler and infinitely more powerful tool than that. He used...

Love.

Bill Gray has been described in many ways: curmudgeonly, combative, aggressive, and cantankerous.

To name but a few. Of course, after a past life as one of Simon de Montfort's murderous thugs in the Albigensian Crusade, he doesn't describe this Love thing in a simpering way:

> To reach those depths of reality it is necessary to "speak the silent tongue", sometimes called the "Old Language", which communicates by means of auto-recognitions of self-states between separate sources of consciousness...
>
> Lovers communicate with each other in this oldest of languages. They need not speak a word or see anything at all. It is enough for them that they feel and know what passes between them. That tells them everything they need to realise whatever concerns them with Cosmic Life. They are living beyond either sounds or sights. Touch-consciousness alone puts them in contact with everything in Existence which relates them with the state of Reality they seek as an integrative identity together.

He goes on to insist that Love opens the gates of life everywhere, and when it is properly applied it will even allow access to the secrets of the humblest stones. But it is no use merely touching our foreheads against the surface of any stone, feeling round it with our fingertips and expecting all sorts of information to come pouring out. What we want, we must go in and get for ourselves. Until we learn how to do this in a spirit of Love for the Life-forces within the stones, they will remain uncommunicative or merely misleading.

It may not be possible to get blood from a stone, but we can obtain communication with life-levels having former or possibly future blood-ties with our world. To attempt this, it is only necessary to establish our physical contact with the stone, and then adjust our Inner attitude of awareness to attune with the objective we seek. It is far from easy to describe this adjustment in words, since it is worked without any.

Gray went into some depth about this energy of Love, and as I sat on a bench yesterday near the Whispering Knights and underlined the stuff I've used here, I was quite moved. When I first read the book in full in 1974 I was too battered and bent out of shape with respect to that 'Love energy' to really appreciate what he was saying.

Lacking his talent and technique, nevertheless I then used Raven to make contact with those stones that were fenced off and uttered (and emoted) my own mawkish attempt at the silent tongue of the 'Old Language': *The people who once made these stones, knew love. And so do I.*

Did anything come roaring or even whispering into my psyche? Not a thing. But there was nothing that I needed or expected, and it felt right to do so, and my lovely, weird wife was happy doing her own stuff at the other side of the field - and it was a perfect day to be out in the sublime countryside. I felt like crying out, as

Eliphas Levi suggested: *I have omnipotence at my command and eternity at my disposal!*

'Let's go to the tea shop along the road,' suggested Margaret when she was done with the Rollright energies. 'You can get a bacon sarnie.'

'I love it when you talk dirty.'

'But stop calling me Nobby, will you?'

(In actual fact neither of us use our given first names.)

A curious aside though…

As I scanned the relevant pages of Bill's book this morning and used some OCR software to make it useable here, only the last line on page 22 went a bit awry. It was presented as:

93 93 93….

Some of the riders behind me will understand that immediately and might have a chuckle. Those who don't, might want to make a little detour somewhere and find out.

Perhaps this is what we need to do with the eidolons of the Templars: send them Love, and in return they might communicate. Or perhaps it's what they need to be released, like Joan Grant's suicide in the subway.

Really, I don't know. Take the reins of my horse whenever you want and steer it where you need to get whatever answers you seek.

***

There was a very marked but amiable presence about the circle yesterday. For some reason it reminded me of a ritual that Paddy had invited me to in her back garden in North Stoke. Bring food, bring drinks to share around, she said. I forgot both and felt like a freeloader. I can't remember now what aim it had but there must have been about 30 folk there, all ages, all backgrounds, all shapes and sizes – like the Rollright stones themselves. Thinking back, it might have been St George's Day, hence April 23rd. Paddy was ex-WRAF (Women's Royal Air Force) where she had known Bill Gray's wife, and so very pro-military, as are Margaret and myself. I do remember her arguing that the original Cross of St George was actually green and not red but I can't add anything more to that. Paddy's son Bob (ex-Coldstream Guard as I recall) took all our watches and we were invited to form a circle outside.

I think that Paddy was the only one who wore a simple robe. The rest of us came as we were, in everyday clothes. Y'see I've never had any desire to wear robes, though I don't knock or mock those who do. As I've always insisted to the 'jobbing wizard' Mike Harris: 'You're not getting *me* into a dress.' Nor do I have any wish or need to stand naked in a cornfield - again, each to their own.

Everyone made a dash outside to be in the West, traditionally the place of Dusk, Water and the Cup. I stood almost alone in the North, the place of Night, Earth and the Stone (or Shield). Although I was given a role – that of my hero Harold Godwinson – and read out my scripted lines with as much verve as I could, I can't remember much more, except that the nasty black dog was leaping all around, even then, and had lots of other people on edge too. I mused that in 1066 the *real* Harold Godwinson might have clubbed the beast.

Just saying.

Like Bill's visit to the Rollrights nothing cosmic or supranatural flowed through my psyche that day. But it was a warm occasion, and amicable, and everyone was determined to do their best and be their best, and although I've attended rituals of a very different kind in which powerful forces did extraordinary things, Paddy's simple ceremony was just as important.

***

Looking back, it makes me wonder today what rituals the Templars might have had. They had their own priests whom we might suppose offered the orthodox rituals and observances. At their trials it did seem that there was this inner core who were wont to worship/adore/touch/kiss the fabled Head. Yet there doesn't seem to have been any hint of esoteric practices such as the Cathars had, which led to the Consolamentum. This was their unique sacrament which enabled the reception of all spiritual gifts, absolution from sin, spiritual rebirth or regeneration, and elevation to a higher plane of awareness. It was this, the highest form of initiation, which enabled them to go singing to the stake.

I'll come back to the adoration of the Head, the Baphomet, later, but I feel again that if I'd been a Templar then at the end of my life I must have thought: *What a waste… I must visit that Carl Jung fella in Zurich when I get to the Other Side.*

If they had been vouchsafed no more than a glimpse of the Baphomet in some appropriate ceremony, what personal impact did it have upon them? It was supposed to be able to make the land fertile (like the Green Man) and various other promises, but it didn't protect its closest worshipers from the most appalling tortures of the Unholy Inquisition. And what use would it be for our Ancuellos herding sheep on the Wiltshire downs?

I'm somewhat reminded of all those cults in the 60s and 70s (and presumably today also) when groups of hopeful aspirants flocked overseas to join the various gurus and god-men that were touting their spiritual wares on the high streets of the Aquarian Age. When the said gurus started buying Rollers and Ferraris and having indiscriminate sex-cum-rape with their wide-eyed disciples, churning out wisdom that had no enduring substance, it eventually sunk in that they were in the hands of snake-oil salesmen. They all began to slink home and hope no-one had noticed. A couple of them even turned up in my life saying, in effect: *We have been to India, and found not what we sought...*

Whenever I think of the Order of the Temple's wealth, I can't get the image of Bernard Madoff out of my mind. This was the man, jailed in 2009, who for years operated the biggest Ponzi scheme in world history. He'd have made a wonderful Grand Master. To get near him you had to belong to the right club – invariably a golf club. You had to have enough money. He would take it all from you and, using the secret wizardry of him and his company, it would increase astonishingly: magickal rates of growth that no other organisation could match. Every dollar made miraculously fertile. Just like the promises behind the Head of Baphomet. In the papal *Articles of Accusation* which detailed the charges against the Templars was stated:

> Item, that they venerated [the Head] as their Saviour
> Item, that they said the Head could save them
> Item, that it could make riches
> Item, that it gave them all the riches of the Order
> Item, that it made the trees flower
> Item, that it made the land germinate

Which is why, after the scam collapsed and the investors lost their life savings, we see heavyweight Hollywood actors making lightweight commercials on British television just to try and recoup their losses.

However, I don't for one moment doubt the sincerity and dedication of Jacques de Molay and his complete commitment to the Templar Mysteries. A few modern commentators make a powerful case for de Molay being regarded at the time as a highly dangerous and threatening Second Messiah. I'll talk about this in a later chapter when I set my fellow-riders free to make their own decisions about. I personally have no axe to grind or sword to wield.

On the whole though, I do think that the group as a whole got a bit dodgy, as every large organisation seems to do over time, no matter how noble their founding principles. If you care to research the very bad behaviour of Templar knights in Scotland toward their tenants, they will lose a bit of the gloss they might have had in your eyes until now.

As Bill Gray said to me as a 17-year-old when it came to joining groups; 'If they're after your money then it's complete rubbish. If they're *not* after your money it might still be complete rubbish but they might be worth a try.'

Alas, the Templars in their heyday were after every penny you had, but you did get some nice underwear in return.

***

I had thought this morning that perhaps my Holy Hiatus and the present musing had taken me too far away from my simple Templar journey. Then I got an email from Jo

Clark, who had accompanied me and Paddy on that first day when I (almost) found the Templar Door.

> A bit like my stand on organised religion I have moved away from organised magical work. I found all the unpleasant backstabbing and false claims, very often by folks who have an exaggerated sense of their own importance, just too much. Now for me, a bit like Paddy, I find there is more magic to be had in a walk in our glorious countryside with my dear gentleman friend Jack (four legged Scottie of course) and the occasional rite done on my own.

I totally agreed. When I told her about this present project and my determination to visit the Temple Church in London, which was the original headquarters of the Order in this country when it was first formed, she added: 'Say a prayer next to the grave of my ancestor William Marshal.'

William Marshal (1147-1219) is regarded by many as the greatest knight who ever lived, and very best of Templars. It would take a book in itself to outline his achievements, so let us make do here with the following from the internet:

> '[Marshal] had also survived the temperament of three of the most notoriously bad-tempered kings in English history. They had required his counsel due to his wisdom and discretion, but most importantly due to his honesty. He reprinted the Magna Carta in his regency, something not often mentioned. Ultimately, William could look towards death proud of his illustrious life and career, and his incredible achievement of honour over money.'

Perhaps Ancuellos is more than just a 'Philip' type possibility but a spin-off from Jo? Or even Paddy, with her military aura?

Hmmm... I say, which is the nearest to the ineffable *Om* that I can intone these days, but serves just as well.

There was more to her email than that, but the rest can wait until we ride toward the Cathars.

***

I promised earlier that I would show you a way to make use of the Templar's splayed cross for your own magick, however you might define it. Honestly, it's the simplest of approaches, as Gray wrote back then.

The following chart was taken from private documents that Bill Gray gave me before his death, which I included in the biography that I co-wrote with Marcus Claridge entitled *The Old Sod: the Odd Life and Inner Work of William G. Gray.*

This table of Correspondences is brilliantly simple and simply brilliant. Here is a chance to make your own Templar Magic. It will have absolutely nothing to do with what Ancuellos might have been involved in, but I promise that it will bring you results.

As shown in that simple illustration here is a way to use the splayed cross to create your own cosmos.

Face to the East; assume an appropriate Templar form, either of Ancuellos or Amberaldus; intone the Motto; change the traditional Archangels with their saints of Longinus, Mauritius, Michael and George, and use this chart to work your awareness around the Quarters.

Don't ask me where you should put those saints. The whole point is that you must make your own connections, via your own research and/or intuition.

If you want to work with others then invite three other people to face inward, assuming the qualities of the Quarters, and you have a complete microcosm. You've even got the 'Words of Power' in the form of the vowel sounds.

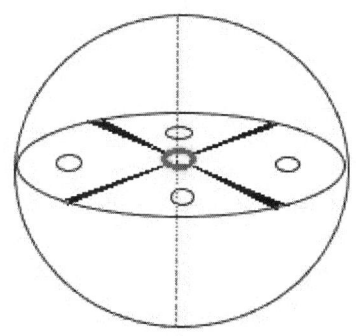

This simple four-fold system is crucial to just about all magick, and Gray's chart is priceless in this respect. The so-called 'Founding Mothers' of modern Wicca, Doreen Valiente and Pat Crowther, whom I knew slightly, were fully aware of this and modified it into their own Craft. As did Evan John Jones.

Personally, I used the major figures from the Arthurian Tradition when I was working in that direction many years ago: Merlin, Arthur, Morgana, Nimue. And later still their equivalents from the Egyptian Mysteries. Plus I was always rather impressed (not to say amused) to hear about the Chaos magickians (sic) in the 1980s using the figures of the Beatles in the Quarters, and even the Spice Girls! I don't know if Chaos Magick is still around today, but it was a breath of fresh air in an era when most aspirants were still bumbling along with the clunky Banishing and Invoking Rituals of the Pentagram, imagining they were cutting edge when they were already a century out of date.

So here it is, with Gray's injunction: *This list can be added to indefinitely. It is recited and acted upon while circumnambulating*

Move on and stop	EAST	SOUTH	WEST	NORTH
Breathe in and out	INHALE	HOLD	EXHALE	EXCLUDE
Call Name	OOOAY	EEEOOO	HOOOAH	HAYEEEE
See the	SUNRISE	NOON	SUNSET	MIDNIGHT
Think of Moon at	NEW	FULL	OLD	DARK
Feel the	SPRING	SUMMER	AUTUMN	WINTER
Greet Archangel	RAPHAEL	MIKAAL	GABRIEL	AURIEL
Experience the Element	AIR	FIRE	WATER	EARTH
Feel	PURE	RADIANT	FLOWING	FERTILE
Feel as if	FLYING	BURNING	SWIMMING	WALKING
Take and use the	SWORD	ROD	CUP	SHIELD
Emote	SORROW	EXCITEMENT	JOY	CONTENTMENT
Use Magnetism to	REPEL	CONTROL	ATTRACT	HOLD
Decide to	WILL	WORK	WANT	WAIT
Have	PERCEPTION	POWER	PURPOSE	PATIENCE
Dedicate	MIND	SPIRIT	SOUL	BODY

And that, I think, is the end of this particular Holy Hiatus. I'm off to bed now with the stone under my pillow and will start riding more directly toward the Templars tomorrow…

Chapter 11

At the Name of...

I've got the Big One coming up soon, with a visit to the Temple Church in London, which was the original headquarters of the Templars in England. But I felt compelled to make a visit to Orchardleigh this morning to take in Matins. I wanted to see again the font with the Green Man, touch Ancuellos' notional grave with my templarish stone, and the small carving of Jesus above the skull, that sits above the aumbry. My plan was that I would use the 'Old Language' as Gray described it, and see if anything would flow through.

I could hardly tell the lovely churchwarden exactly why I was there in case he thought me a nutter, or worse still a Black Magician. To the masses not in this line of inner work, anyone they don't understand is always a *Black* Magician. Builders in our house, when we first moved in, saw my collection of books and almost ran out the door. Which is ridiculous really as most of them are about the origins and mysteries of Jesus, from all sorts of unusual and often opposing angles. Mind you I hate the ridiculous term '*White* Magician' just as much. Was Torquemada of the Spanish Inquisition a 'white' Christian or a 'black' one? What would *he* say? These questions of Light and Darkness have been bothering me a lot lately, and they are fundamental to an understanding of both Templars and Cathars, as I hope to show.

The churchwarden was delightful, and was pleased to show me around, inside and out, before the service. He showed me the graves next to the lake of Sir Henry Newbolt and his wife, but I didn't ask where the third member of the ménage was buried. He took me through the wondrous Priest's Door in the north wall but too fast for me to try and get a sense of liminality. And he showed me the ornate aumbry, a small recess in the wall which would have housed the sacraments. He was particularly impressed that it still had its oak door, as most of these were torn off during the Reformation to make sure that no precious items were being hidden. I touched the figure of Jesus above the skull. Did anything flow through from the 'Old Language'? Not a thing.

Above all these he was particularly proud and somewhat perplexed by the appearance of beavers and their young that had been busy doing whatever it is the beavers do with trees and water around the lake. Beavers became extinct in Britain 400 years ago and it is only recently that a few were reintroduced in faraway Devon to see if they would breed, and study what effect they might have on the bio-diversity of their new habitat. My guide had no idea how this family had suddenly appeared at the lake island of Orchardleigh. He was rather delighted by the size of the tree they had brought down.

Hmmm again. Apparently if beavers appear in dreams then according to the Native American traditions you are being offered great wisdom. As a holy animal it may be expressing innate or unconscious information or insights you have that are becoming conscious. The lesson is that we must believe in our dreams as if they were real, and build on our dreams as if they are already our reality.

I can do that. I'm already doing that. My actual night dreams are absurd enough as they are without talking beavers entering into them, but the creatures do seem to fit neatly into my waking dreamscape around this particular site.

I have to mention the actual service because it will become relevant when I try to make sense of the Templars and their attitude to Jesus. Bear with me...

The occasion was beautiful. Having no electricity the church was lit by about 50 large candles as it must have been when it was first built. A modern log-burning stove churned out enough heat to make the congregation comfortable. The place as actually packed by young couples who had to prove their commitment to the church by regular attendance for a certain number of weeks. Once married, I doubt if any of them would ever come again. Without the beauty of the setting, St Mary's church on the island in the lake would become another redundant church like the one at Alton Priors. Apart from the engaged couples, there were only six other folk, all of them older than me.

The stained glass windows cannot easily be seen from outside, but I wanted to get a look at the Agnus Dei. And there it was, glowing by candlelight, and the Cross of St George it carried had a marked green colour, just as Paddy had said. I couldn't get near to see if this was a trick of the light.

There is clearly a tormented, frustrated ex-Benedictine within me. It must be a past life thing. Margaret is the same. We sit quietly in ancient empty churches, as I said before, and can – sometimes – feel real peace. Once, in Quarr Abbey when we listened to the monks doing plainsong, we both burst into tears. As for the rest of it, the actual day-to-day reality of Churchianity leaves us both cold.

I listened to the churchwarden reading out the Apostles' Creed.

> I believe in God, the Father almighty,
> creator of heaven and earth.
> I believe in Jesus Christ, God's only Son, our Lord,
> who was conceived by the Holy Spirit,
> born of the Virgin Mary,
> suffered under Pontius Pilate,
> was crucified, died, and was buried;
> he descended to the dead.
> On the third day he rose again;
> he ascended into heaven,
> he is seated at the right hand of the Father,
> and he will come to judge the living and the dead.
> I believe in the Holy Spirit,
> the holy catholic Church,
> the communion of saints,
> the forgiveness of sins,
> the resurrection of the body,
> and the life everlasting. Amen.

Alas, I don't believe any of it. Not a single Word. But don't let that put you off, because I'm not out to convert my fellow travellers into any one system of belief or disbelief.

I sneaked out when the service was over, before I got collared by anyone and my mild but insistent sociopathy kicked in. Y'see basically I just have to escape from people. My gorgeous daughters all have duct tape at hand when I visit to keep me in place. The only person I'm completely comfortable with, all the time, and with whom I never get bored or distracted is Margaret. I used to describe myself as hermit-type, but that's not *quite* true. Mind you, perhaps I'm being a bit cavalier with the use of the term 'sociopath', thinking this might be better than 'miserable old git'. I've just googled the traits and they come out as:

- Glibness and Superficial Charm.
- Manipulative and Cunning. They never recognize the rights of others and see their self-serving behaviours as permissible. ...
- Grandiose Sense of Self. ...
- Pathological Lying. ...
- Lack of Remorse, Shame or Guilt. ...
- Shallow Emotions. ...
- Incapacity for Love.
- Need for Stimulation.

Is this my own answer to the Apostle's Creed? I'll hold my hand up to two of those and if you ever meet me for me for a cuppa tea on some neutral ground then I'll tell you which. Just let me escape after an hour and we'll get on brilliantly.

On the way out, on the long drive to the main road, through the golf course then open parkland, I felt a powerful connection between Raven (who had been lurking in the shadows of the car) and the dryads of the magnificent trees.

(However, Margaret was reading the above over my shoulder and she's just wacked me with a rolled-up copy of Nexus. 'Eejit,' she says, being brilliant with regional accents and numerous languages. 'A socio*path* is a mad axe-man. The word you want is socio*phobe*. That means something quite different.' Well, if she says so.)

***

I'm writing this in Trowbridge Library again and I realise that I'm being sucked back toward faery again. In fact I read a small item about the Templars last night which made me raise an eyebrow: one of the accusations made against before their rapid demise was that they had gone native in Outremer, and absorbed so many mystical ideas and practises from their supposed enemies that they had become 'fairy Muslims'!

So let's try to outline my own attitude toward Jesus now lest it corrupt whatever understanding I might try and glean for/from Ancuellos.

I've written several books on purely pagan topics but do accept that Jesus did exist as an historical figure. While I loathe the depredations of the Holy Roman Catholic Church I'm quite happy to accept that Jesus was an unusual fella and certainly married to the Magdalen. In fact there's a particular piece of music which always triggers off a vision of him and Mary, sitting at a table, planning what to do next. This seems to have been just before the entry into Jerusalem. No more than that, and the vision never moves on. They were a nice couple. I liked them. I think we could have become friends. Human, all too human, both of them.

***

Yet I had a strange experience some years ago which I still cannot explain and which may or may not be relevant. I'd had a fairly hefty operation at the local hospital under the care of the excellent NHS surgeons. I should have been home after 6 days, but in the wee small hours of the final morning I had a very bad reaction to one of the new hefty painkillers they gave me, and spent the day in extreme pain and semi-comatose. I don't criticise the hospital for this: if I had had a spoonful of shandy the alcohol would make me twitchy all next day. So the effect of the di-hyper-doodah was not to be wondered at.

Anyway, I really thought I was on my way out. I could barely speak. My temperature must've been close to Fahrenheit 451, my blood pressure was going off the scale, and they were talking about moving me into the intensive care unit. I knew then, that after about 12 hours of non-stop misery I had to call for help. As best as I can explain it, I said out loud: 'May the White Christ come to me; I need to be healed in order to Serve.'

I dunno where the White Christ thingy came from. It was a spontaneous outburst rather than a religious one. I said it three times.

Within seconds I heard the nurse at door of the ward call out: 'The Hospital Chaplain's here! Anyone want to see him?'

I was too crocked to be able to call through the curtains around my bed and say Yes. But then, if he had come, what would I have done? Open a rheumy eye and say: 'Are you the White Christ? Can you heal me?' He'd have thought me a mad! Actually, on reflection, I think if I *had* done that, then something might have been enabled whether the Chaplain wanted it or not, as he'd have become a conduit of sorts.

Instead the moment passed, but a very short while after that the strangest thing happened. It was as though 'someone' standing to my right gave a Homer Simpson-ish *Doh*! of exasperation at my not acting when I had the chance and decided to step in. It was as though this Being grabbed me by the back of my neck, hauled my soul out of my body and duffed it face down on the bottom of the mattress as I watched, bashing it up and down as you would to empty an ashtray. And then shoved it back in, with the very clear words: 'In ten minutes your body will start to work normally.'

And bugger me - it did. When the doctors came in *en masse* to see whether I should go to the Intensive Care Unit, they were bewildered to see me sitting up quite happily and ready to go home.

I don't know what really happened there. I won't knock it.

Wendy Berg, who wrote the brilliant and ground-breaking book *Red Tree, White Tree: Faeries and Humans in Partnership* reckons it must have been a faery thing. I've since been told by others people who work in the Faery Traditions that some of these shining ones have a belief in a White Christ, while others have none at all. In the Hebrides, however, the Viking raiders and settlers used this as a term of scorn: their god, Thor, was red; their calling the Christ 'White' was rather like calling someone 'yellow': it was an insult.

There are moments when the concept of a 'White Christ' brings a sort of peace within me. Yet make no mistake, whatever it was that grabbed ahold of me in the hospital was not the 'gentle Jesus meek and mild'. This Being was prickly, uncompromising, capable of exasperation and hiding between shadows. The Jesus of the Apostles' Creed this was most emphatically *not*.

I even think this might be a book I might attempt some day: *A Search for the White Christ*. Gawd knows where that will take me!

I'll assume that anyone still with me will have ideas of their own as regards this concept of 'Christ', so I'll spur my destrier and ride us toward what might be the equal concept of Baphomet.

When the Templars were being tortured they were made to confess to worshipping a deity they called Baphomet. Confusingly, this took on different forms:

An idol with a human skull
A head with two faces
A head with a beard - without a beard
With the head of a cockerel
With the head of a man
With the head of a goat and the body of a man
With wings and cloven feet
The upper body of a woman
A candle on its head

I get a horrific sense of the Inquisitors here and I'm reminded of the so-called Satanic Abuse trials in South Ronaldsay in the 1990s. Children were taken into care and families broken up because impressionable social workers created a veritable witch-hunt. The leader of these, who led the interviews, was later described by several of the children as a terrifying figure who was 'fixated on finding satanic abuse'. Other children described how she urged them to draw circles and faces, presumably as evidence indicating abusive rites. One of the children later said of the interviews: 'In order to get out of a room, after an hour or so of saying, "No, this never happened", you'd break down.' Children concerned had been separated and subjected to repeated cross-examinations almost as if the aim was to force confessions rather than to assist in therapy. When it came to court the judge threw the cases out and severely censured all those officials concerned, pointing out the absurdity of their 'evidence'.

In September 2006 it was announced that one person, who had been 8 years old when she was taken into care by social workers in November 1990, was given legal aid to sue the council. She said that she had been the victim of a modern-day witch hunt by overzealous and possibly unbalanced social workers determined to break up her family. She said that the interview techniques used at the time were designed to break the children down, and that she was bribed with sweets to tell social workers what they wanted to hear.

You get the point. As I said much earlier, if I'd been a Templar undergoing torture, I'd tell them whatever they wanted to hear just to get them to stop. And likewise the above descriptions of 'Baphomet' probably owe more to the darkness within their Inquisitors and what they wanted to hear, than what actually happened within the Order.

It just struck me now, at the end of my working life and into happy retirement that I've been lucky. Although I trained as a teacher and did a couple of years at the coal-face, so to speak, I was never able to get back into the profession despite innumerable applications. Yet if I had, there is no doubt that at some point worried parents would have found out about my 'other' inner side and the cry 'Black Magician!' would ring down the corridors. Then nothing I could say would persuade them otherwise. I would have been forced out. I think this actually happened to the late Gerald Suster when parents or governors found out that he was an authority on Aleister Crowley. So, considering that all I've ever wanted to do since I was 5 was write weird books that some people might find useful, I think now in looking back that I've always been under some sort of protection.

But I'm burbling again… or is it a whinge-boast?

***

So if the term Christ simply comes from the Greek word Christos, meaning 'anointed one' or 'chosen one', what does Baphomet mean?

Idries Shah in his book *The Sufis* argued:

> Western scholars have recently supposed that 'Bafomet' has no connection with Mohammed, but could well be a corruption of the Arabic *abufihamat* (pronounced in the Moorish Spanish something like *bufihimat*). The word means 'father of understanding'. In Arabic, 'father' is taken to mean 'source, chief seat of', and so on. In Sufi terminology, *ras el-fahmat* (head of knowledge) means the mentation of man after undergoing refinement - the transmuted consciousness.

On the other hand the scholar Hugh Schonfield detected within the name a first-century Jewish code called the Atbash cipher, which was used to conceal the names of individuals. This code appears in the Dead Sea Scrolls, and in modern Freemasonry, and when applied to the Templar word 'Baphomet' it reveals the word 'Sophia' - the Greek for wisdom. However, it more specifically means female wisdom. Sophia as Goddess of Wisdom not only appears in the Old Testament (as the translation of the Hebrew 'Chokmah') but was also important to many Gnostic sects.

In terms of the Kabbalah, which needn't distract us here, the so-called Magical Image of Chockmah is said to possess two *partzufim* ('faces'): the higher being referred to as *Abba Ila'ah* ('the higher father'), whereas the lower is referred to as *Yisrael Saba* ('Israel, the Elder'). These two *faces* are referred to jointly as *Abba* ('father'). Just as interrogators on South

151

Ronaldsay saw the little girl's two Nativity masks as evidence of diabolic rituals, could the 'Head with two faces' be of this nature? Was some innocent Templar simply trying, as his fingernails were being ripped out, to explain something of the spiritual nature of Baphomet?

Christopher Knight and Robert Lomas, two high-grade Freemasons discuss the actual head known as Baphomet and insist that the Templars performed the same ritual as that used as the 3rd Degree in Freemasonry, and they must have had a supply of skulls and of long white burial shrouds in which to wrap their candidates.

> As Freemasons, we are not at all surprised that the Templars had human heads because a skull and crossed thigh bones are still used in the Masonic living resurrection ceremony that has Templar origins. If any Freemason today was asked if he belonged to a cult that worshipped human heads he would think the questioner quite mad, and yet a quick calculation leads us to believe that Freemasonry around the world probably possesses a total of some fifty thousand skulls!

The arguments among modern Templarists, if I can coin a term, flow thick and fast as to whether this was the actual preserved head of John the Baptist, Huges de Payens or even Jesus. I'll come back to this later.

***

Then again you can't avoid the monstrous Baphomet that was envisaged by the legendary Eliphas Levi (1810-1875). This figure is hermaphroditic, with a pair of female breasts and the alchemical SOLVE and COAGULA upon the forearms, meaning separate and unite respectively. It has two crescent moons, one light and one dark, behind each hand. A torch on the head and a caduceus rising from the groin area. In fact I can't find fault with the symbolism. It is all to do with the unification of opposites, male-female, good-evil, waxing-waning, day-night. Levi called it a pantheistic and  magical figure of the Absolute, and I can't disagree. Although Levi created this within his own lifetime it has somehow stuck into the modern consciousness as likely to be *the* Baphomet for whom the Templars were willing to serve and die.

I described Levi's image as monstrous, and so it is, but on the other hand I find the sight of a wounded, tortured man nailed to a cross an equally monstrous sight.

 And there is also the mysterious Abraxas to be considered, as the symbol of this very odd Being is found on the seal of Grand Master of the Temple in Paris, and was certainly used in a French charter in 1214. This figure consists of a male warrior with a cockerel's head, human arms and snakes as legs. He carries a shield and whip, perhaps, and is encircled by the words *Secretum Templi*. Apparently this particular description of Abraxas was known as Anguipede, which means 'snake-foot'. When Jung wrote his *Seven Sermons to the Dead* which released the tormented spirits in his living room, he referred to Abraxas as *the* power above all, the First Principle and the ruler of 365 heavens.

However I don't believe that this would have meant *anything* to our Ancuellos, still standing with his back to the doorway at Alton Priors in 1307 and wondering what the hell was happening to his Order. As French writers Jean Robin and Georges Cagger opine:

> The Order of the Temple was indeed constituted of seven 'exterior' circles dedicated to the minor mysteries, and of three 'interior' circles corresponding to the initiation into the great mysteries. And the 'nucleus' was composed of those seventy Templars 'interrogated' by Clement V [after the arrests of 1307].

I tend to see Ancuellos as belonging to the outer court of the Order and, as a mere sheep-herder, likely to have been bewildered by the esoterica given above. Being virtually exiled into the heart of Wiltshire, standing unwittingly before the great cosmic interplay of the Earth Mysteries being enacted upon the hills at every season, I fancy that he (or his historical equivalent) was by now totally despondent, desperately wanting to go home and yet not daring to do so.

      Poor poor bugger…

On the other hand there was a notable carving on the Templar Commandery in Saint Bris-le-Vineux which sports a rather jolly Horned God that would have been quite recognisable to the common folk of

154

Wiltshire. Would he have had some hint of this kind of Being even in the outer circle of the Order?

And, as an afterthought, can we give our avatar an actual place of origin in order to energise him more? That is, can we imagine that might he have come from Saint Bris-le-Vineux, in the heart of France?

No, if we are to create a home anywhere then it has to be in the one place I rather hesitate to mention, associated with the one name I don't even want to explain.

The fact is, I had a rotten night last night with a thumping headache and every tube and vessel from my shoulders upward in distress. I was up at 2.30 and reading a (comparatively relaxing) book about the last battle of the Great War to distract myself from the energies/thoughts/half-dreams. I'm not keeping my templarish stone under the pillow any more. Margaret is away in Gomorrah this week and it's a good job she is because she'd tell me off and blame the Bloody Templars, as she now thinks of them, for my distress.

So I'm going to say two names to you and let you ride off on your own if you want and find an appropriately named book by the major adept Gareth

The faery Melusine of Lusignan

Knight on Amazon. This might illumine more about the link between Faery and Templars than I can ever fathom. Don't ask me to explain more. Don't ask me to help you out if you're taken in strange directions. All I want to do for the next chapter is talk about the Light and Dark and the good guys known as the Cathars, who are somehow

155

intimately connected with the Templars – and in indirect ways with Wiltshire also.

And the two names I will give you now before I gallop off in a different direction and crash somewhere are:

Lusignan.
and
Melusine.
Now don't get lost…

Chapter 12

The Good People

I wish I'd met Arthur Guirdham. I saw him coming out the Botanical Gardens in Bath's Royal Victoria Park but I was too shy to introduce myself. At one point, for several years, if I had walked across the fields from my house in Winsley, I could have dropped into his house in Bathford on the edge of the same plateau. I have often rehearsed the missed opportunity but I'm not sure what I could have said. Instead I wrote to him, as I did to so many others, but my letters were little better than adoring fan mail of the sort he could have done without. He always replied graciously.

When I stumbled upon his *The Cathars and Reincarnation* I was deeply moved. I have never had any sense that I may have had a past life as a Bonshomme as the Cathars were called. Their attraction for me was simply that the Cathar beliefs were so simple, so black-and-white, so pure, that after a lifetime of working my way through the Hermetic systems it gave me a chance to remove all sorts of clunky, heavy, presumably protective armours.

He also wrote The *Lake and the Castle* in 1976 which talked more about group reincarnation, this time involving Celtic Christians. Again, I never had any sense that I might have been part of this faction either because I was already, by this time, heavily involved in my own saga of group reincarnation relating to Lindisfarne and a figure called Yvius. Who may or may not have been me. I've even got letters from Dame Felicitas Corrigan who helped me with that one! Although allow me a little digression here…

***

Now that I'm on the last lap, so to speak, I don't cling to any hard and fast beliefs about reincarnation these days. Without getting sucked into the (to me) tedious philosophies and speculations about linear time and all the rest, I act 'as if' the traditional concepts of reincarnation are real. It makes yarning and everyday conversation considerably easier. Whether there *are* such things as previous lives or 'other lives' in which everything is happening at once, I really don't know and there are lots of things I can't explain and no longer agonise about. I have had numerous seers 'read the records' for me but not one of them has agreed. Odd things have happened which have suggested past lives (none of them of any status) and while I have gone with the flow and tone of these I have nothing invested in them.

***

Yet Guirdham's writings, in a sense, gave me a degree of comfort. The countless synchronicities which sprang up around me and my life, which overlapped or echoed with him and his, are not relevant here. Bizarrely enough, my concerns with my own saga of (what seemed to be) group reincarnation are also tied in with the environs of Bath. I wrote something about the latter in my light-hearted *Me, mySelf and Dion Fortune*. Once, in Tescos in Trowbridge, I met an elderly lady with whom I had worked years before. As we reminisced about our time as care-workers in the Winsley Centre she had what seemed a mini seizure and inserted broken words in her sentence: 'the doctor…Guirdham…he started having visions at Conkwell Green.. about medieval France...' Then she stopped, shook her head and carried on with her original very mundane yarn. It was almost like an instant possession. *What was that about the doctor?* I asked. *And Conkwell Green?* She had no idea what I meant.

Even people in Conkwell wouldn't have known exactly where Conkwell Green is, and it was/is a profoundly important area to me personally. I had picked up a very strong inner contact with the Horned God there, at the Spring of the Green Man, which led to my books *Earth God Rising* and even (long story this one) *The Inner Guide to Egypt.* So I suppose one thing Dr. Guirdham gave me as a young man was this sense of Spirit of Place, which forms my own personal Mystery.

***

Would Ancuellos have known, or known of, the Bonshommes as they were called? Waving his sword about, protecting his sheep, might he have looked back at his time in France and thought he had made the wrong choice? In his excellent book *The Head of God*, Keith Laidler reflects on the close links between Templars and Cathars and adds about the latter that:

> Their conception of Christ reflected this world-view [that] Jesus had been sent into the world in order to redeem these lost angelic souls from the confines of matter, and to return them to their 'natural' abode with the Good God. But, unlike the Roman Church, while most Cathars greatly revered Jesus, they still regarded him as distinctly human. A man filled with the spirit of

the Good God, but a man nevertheless. In some cases, this was conceived as a heavenly Christ within the earthly Jesus, who had been begotten normally as other men. Accordingly, the Cathars repudiated the dogma of the virgin birth. They also discounted the crucifixion and the cross. The resurrection in the body was ridiculed; the Cathars preferred (as in many mystery religions) to regard 'resurrection' as a rebirth that came about during life, as a result of union with God. The apocryphal *Gospel of Philip* casts scorn on the 'bodily resurrectionists' and states the Gnostic position clearly: 'Those who say they will die first and then rise are in error. If they do not receive the resurrection while they live, when they die they will receive nothing.' Many of these beliefs echo the accusations brought against the Templars when they were accused of heresy, and may indicate a close connection between the doctrines of the two groups.

The Cathar priests were known as the Parfaits, or perfected ones. They had received the Consolamentum that I mentioned earlier. Parfaits could be of either sex and many were married, though they eschewed sexual relations. They travelled in pairs and – unlike the ostentations of the Catholic Church - they held their services in barns or ordinary houses or in the open air. Some authorities, and I think Guirdham himself, said that the Parfaits wore a cord under their garments tied around the waist next to their skin – very similar to the cord said to have been worn by the Templars. They were generally known as the *Bonshommes* or Good People, and I think that they were exactly that. Even Saint Bernard, while not condoning their ideas, could find no fault with their behaviour.

Even at the height of the Albigensian Crusade, when a pre-incarnation of Bill Gray was doing his worst among the innocents, the Templars sheltered fugitive Cathars and there are numerous examples of them giving succour and sanctuary to knights who actively fought for the pacifist Cathars against the crusaders.

Not that this makes it any easier for me to clarify my own ideas about the Templars and Cathars. I think that the riders behind me, still clinging on, should try to grab what they can as we gallop past. Personally I take some comfort from the words of the Benedictine Abbot Dom John Chapman who wrote in his 'Spiritual Letters' that all spiritual writers disagreed with one another and that he disagreed with all of them. If anything, trying to give some shape or substance to Ancuellos is helping me give shape to my own Light and Darkness and the little fiddly bits in my psyche that can resonate to both.

***

Jo Clark, the descendant of William Marshal, who was also my 'Best Man' at our wedding, is a real historian who searches proper archives with a gimlet eye - unlike me who just does some cut-and-pastery from the internet. The rest of her email to me went into a little more detail about the Cathars:

> In 1283 Edmund of Cornwall, nephew of King Henry III founded and endowed the College of Bonhommes at Ashridge, near Berkhamsted, Hertfordshire for the purpose of guarding a holy relic, the blood of Christ, which he divided between there and Hailes Abbey. He brought a small number of brethren to it, reputedly from France, and known as Bonhommes. Later the

monastery was re-endowed by Edward the Black Prince, establishing the foundation as one of importance for both piety and pilgrimage and of increasing wealth and landownership. In 1352 he founded a further house of Bonhommes at Edington.

The Bonhommes, who wore an ash gray habit, represented a new Order for England, and are considered to have had Cathar affiliations, with seven priest brethren at Ashridge and abour eighteen at Edington, and served in accordance with the rule of St Augustine. It has been stated that this was the only house of this order in England, except the small college at Edington in Wiltshire.

Edington is just down the road from us. We have many Danish friends via Margaret's connection with the European Commission in Brussels. When they visit, I make a point of taking them to see where the Battle of Ethandun was fought, when the army of Alfred the Great defeated the Great Heathen Army led by the Dane warlord Guthrum in May 878 and laid the basis of us becoming English.

Edington's massive Priory was founded in the 14th century and became a monastery of the Brothers of Penitence, or Bonhommes. Its large church continues in use as the parish church of St Mary, All Saints and St Katherine, but the other monastery buildings were destroyed by 1579.

Remember I yarned in an earlier chapter about sights seen from afar that you make a mental note to visit one day? Well Edington is one of them. Another long story but St Katherine is as important to me as the other energies of Mary and the All Saints were to the Templars.

Thank you for that Jo…

But now my neck is crippling me again and I've got to ready for tomorrow. I need to lie on the couch and absorb myself in a good Western – or better still *The Quiet Man*, large parts of which I know by heart.

Chapter 13

At the Head Quarters

I had a nice surprise on the train into London today. My cousin Joyce was in the same carriage, going to see her daughter. And she'd been reading on her i-pad thingy my novel *The Movie Star*, which is set in Dorsetshire in the 1930s, and is an outright and non-mystical love story based loosely on Robin Hood.

'I'm thoroughly enjoying it Alan' she said. 'It's so well written.'

I kissed her hand.

'Apart from Margaret, you're the only person I know who has ever read it. You've made yer old cousin a *very* happy man…'

This, dear reader, is what is known in psycho-spiritual-literary terms as a hint. Anyone who ever buys a copy, in any format, will get a free mug of tea if ever we meet.

***

I wore my Templar ring on the middle finger of my left hand. No occult significance in this, as it's the only one it will fit, given my gnarly digits. The ring was given to me by the late Marcia Pickands. This is the lady who Bill Gray (that name again!) thought was Dion Fortune reborn. Marcia herself thought that too. Then he changed his mind and so did Marcia, feeling it was all down to a very powerful overshadowing, such as I had had for years with dear old 'Bert'. I never actually questioned or challenged Marcia about this because it just wasn't important. I accept people for who they are *now*, not who they might have been. My memory is somewhat hazy but I think she was also described as a 'White Dragon' expert in kung-fu, or some related discipline, and taught strangleholds and death-grips to trainees of the CIA. She was fun, and kind, and very much the real thing magickally speaking. She had all the gifts you would want to find in a genuine adeptus but used them for healing.

Of course I turned in the wrong direction as soon as I left Waterloo Station. Fortunately some kind soul in the city, knowing I was on my way, had obviously spent all night putting up large maps at every other lamppost, with the words YOU ARE HERE writ large especially. It was a lovely day so I was quite happy to stroll along and cross Blackfriars Bridge. In 1982 Roberto Calvi dubbed 'God's banker' because of his work with the utterly corrupt Vatican, was found hanging from scaffolding. Bricks had been stuffed in his pockets and he had more than £10,000 in cash on him. In the months before his death he had been accused of stealing millions being laundered on behalf of the mafia. One of the most influential figures in the Calvi story was Licio Gelli, once Grand Master of the P2 masonic lodge of which Silvio Berlusconi had been a member. Gelli was sentenced to 12 years for fraud in connection with the collapse of Calvi's own bank. I bet they fancied themselves as modern-day Templars within *that* lodge.

Minutes later I was twiddling the Templar ring as I entered the impressive precincts of the Inns of Court, which are the professional associations for barristers in England and Wales. All barristers must belong to one such association.

To my shock as I turned into one of the courtyards I was immediately faced by a very limber young man in shorts doing impossible and nearly obscene things with his legs: kicking his right foot above his head and clutching it with his left hand; ditto with the other leg. It was like watching a male version of those sheela-na-gigs that Ancuellos would have perved at in local churches. To those who don't know what these are, the Sheela-na-gig is a carving of a naked female with the legs wide apart and the hands opening her cunt. He saw my discomfiture and smiled.

'Enjoy,' he said, as he put his legs together and set off for his jog as everyone else seemed to be doing on that May morning. I bet his drove an Audi and belonged to a golf club.

Funny how times change. In my home town of Ashington, coming of age in the 60s and 70s, nobody jogged. Nobody. No-one even touched their toes unless they'd had seven pints.

The Temple Church, which is large but actually somewhat dwarfed by the secular buildings around was at least open for me this time. I'd half expected the storms I described earlier on my first abortive visit. Maybe the Templars are beginning to warm to me. I paused at the front door for a moment and got unto my astral gear, if I can call it that. ('Assumption of the God-form' is the technical term, but I think that's a presumption too far, even for me.) So I entered, visualising myself in the style of Amberaldus – that is, as a Grand Master of the Temple who would have done his stuff here in the 13th Century. I rather hoped that sensitive souls would 'see' this and bend their heads in obeisance. The two behind the desk looked at me hard. Did they see my splendid, shimmering astral vestments? No, they were making an instant assessment as to whether to charge me £5 ordinary, or £3 for a senior. To my astonishment it didn't take them more than a second to apply the latter.

I must have been standing in a bad light.

The church was impressive in a cool, almost austere way. I headed straight toward the prone stone figure of William Marshal, Earl of Pembroke, touched his brow, his ajna chakra, with my templarish stone and thanked him, and sang the praises of his great-great-multiple-greats descendant Jo Clark. I noticed there were fresh flowers at his feet, and that it was his birthday on May 20th.

Really, he was regarded here as a major figure, the greatest of the Templars, an exemplar of what a Templar Knight could have been – and actually was, in his case. When he was still a young man he was said to have bested over 500 knights in tournaments. Although he stayed loyal to the notoriously bad King John, he was central to negotiations which led to the latter signing the Magna Carta at Runnymede in 1215. This was the first formal document which stated that a King had to follow the laws of the land and it guaranteed the rights of individuals against the wishes of the King. An astonishing piece of legislation at that time. On John's death in 1216 Marshal was appointed Guardian of England in order to support John's heir, the boy-king Henry III. Making sure that nothing was going to slip, Marshal re-issued the Magna Carta twice more in his lifetime and so endured its survival. In 1217 Louis of France claimed the English crown for himself and invaded. The good Earl of Pembroke, now aged over 70, led the forces which defeated them at the Battle of Lincoln.

By this time all the bits and pieces of my body from the neck up were giving me gyp. Margaret, as I think I said, calls it my 'Templar Head' and I'm inclined to agree by now. Still, in the heart of one of the biggest and busiest cities in the world I was able to sit in absolute silence and peace on one of the seats and put head into my hands to wait for it to pass, while 'peeping and muttering' what I needed to say to any Beings around or within. A priest came out in a long red dress and lit two candles. According to the web-site there was going to be a 'Holy Communion (said)' soon, but I didn't want to stay for that and wasn't sure what it even meant. There were three other tourists around the edges of the church and I suppose he saw me as the only one actually worshipping. From my posture, head in hands, he must have thought I was a soul in torment and needed succour. In fact, all I really wanted was a couple of paracetamol. I think he was going to come over but I upped and left.

One thing that struck me amid all the (modern-ish) stained glass and very ancient tiling on the upper level, was that there were Agnus Deis in abundance, mothers with child, various saintly looking fellas, the expected Templar crosses, and (for some reason) numerous examples of Pegasus. This was explained in a leaflet as symbolising virtue and creative inspiration, as would be used in all the Inns of Court; conspiracy theorists argue that it is not Pegasus at all, but a covert reference to Buraq, the winged steed which took Muhammad to various heavens.

I couldn't see a single image of the crucifixion. If there was one, it was exceedingly well hidden.

***

There were a lot of flags out around London yesterday because of the Royal Wedding tomorrow. The notion of Sacred Marriages and the sought-after *hieros-gamos,* where human participants enact the sexual relationship between a god and goddess and at the moment of climax experience gnosis/transcendence – whatever their highest aspirations are - has real fascination for me.

I don't for one moment believe that the noble House of Windsor (more accurately known as the House of Saxe-Coburg-Gotha) has any 'special' blood within it. I don't think anyone has, not even that fella Jesus. Research has shown recently that that although certain unlikely things can be passed down via DNA the effect peters out after a couple of generations. I am certain that my present detestation of mud comes from what my grandfather experienced in the trenches in Flanders during the Great War. Which rather wipes out half the impact of the present-day best-sellers relating to the Templars and Sacred Bloodlines.

Thinking of flags and the symbolism of the Templars' holy Beausant, I cut and pasted a piece about that from some web page that I've since lost, but here it is anyway:

> Among the symbolists, it is generally accepted that the banner reflects the duality of the world. There is a dark, evil, and bitterly frightening side; yet, there is a beautiful, pleasant, and glorious side as well. The black is on top because in this world of sin and transgressions, evil seems to hold sway. However, underneath, the good is ever present and will, in the fullness of time, correct every form of error and bring to justice those who have committed vile and impious acts toward God and toward man. The

banner, thus interpreted, was bright and beautiful to friends of Christ, but dark and dreadful to His enemies.

Because I'm not a Templar, and still doubt that I've ever been one in a previous life, I can challenge that. Darkness is not in itself Evil, any more than Light is always and ineffably Good. Spend a little time thinking about this: darkness is profoundly necessary to our well-being and very existence. If you doubt that, spend tonight trying to sleep with all the lights on. Think hard for more crucial examples...

Many years ago I did a lot of work with the Billie-John, and also Judith Page, regarding the Egyptian *neter* of Set, who has always been the fall-guy, the scape-goat. Yet I always found Set's pure energies healing, and protective. Perhaps on my hospital bed I should have called out 'May the Black Christ come to me...'?

Just a thought.

The name Beausant itself seems to be an obvious composite of two French words that even I with my 63% Duo-Lingo abilities can fathom. Apparently the word 'seant' signified in medieval times the state of becoming, and modern Templarists feel that the whole word is best interpreted as 'Be Glorious'. That is, an expectation that they would conduct themselves bravely in battle and be generous in victory.

I think I missed a trick by not entering Temple Church waving an astral Beausant. One of the ways of making contact with inner plane Orders is by visualising their particular symbols and sending it out during your meditations like the searchlight they used in Gotham City to contact Batman. As a teen I spent many a night projecting the (now-forgotten) symbol of the (now defunct) Order of the Pyramid and Sphinx into the aethyrs, but that's another story. Sometime soon I'll create a path-working for myself involving the astral form of Ancuellos, on a high hill, waving the Beausant with a view to attracting like-minded souls. You might like to try that yourselves.

***

So did anything happen when I touched William Marshal's brow?

Not a thing.

I wondered later on the train on the way back whether I should have used that wonderful Templar graffiti of the hand with a heart on its palm. Maybe I'll create a visualisation involving that, but I'd need to check first whether the symbol of the heart in the 13th Century meant exactly the same as today, because I tend to doubt that.

Although it is not *exactly* accurate to say nothing happened. For example, I didn't have an explosion of insight when cousin Joyce appeared next to me in the train but there was certainly a sense of 'rightness' between us. Same with William Marshal. I needed to make the physical contact with the stone and would have gone away distressed if I hadn't. I accepted long ago that in many areas I am 'psychically thick', almost as though I have a thick protective armour to keep out the immediacy of certain energies/entities. I've always had a guarded envy of those whose psychic gifts I admire, trust and make ruthless use of, but in truth I couldn't have coped. I outlined something of this in my quasi-autobiography *Sex and Light.* That is also an occult hint.

However, what often happens is that the energies tend to drip through my everyday consciousness in ways that I need to make sense of them. That is, they 'go live' often long after that original contact. Unusually I had a very lucid and relevant dream that very night in which I found myself standing before a range of Alpine peaks. A couple of others were with me, standing behind but unseen. I had the sense that I had led them here toward this (apparently) impossible barrier.

'Am I supposed to cross these peaks?' I asked.

'You will be helped,' said a woman's voice.

'By whom?'

'They will come to help you. They are soldiers from another dimension. They will come with shields.'

I woke immediately and scribbled this down on the pad next to my bed. While that was a very powerful and intriguing statement I won't get too excited. Over the entirety of my long life I've had many such directed at me from all sorts of sources. Some of them seemed instantly nonsensical but proved themselves much later. Others were immediately profound yet quickly showed to have no substance. Perhaps this will be like the prophetic, apparently meaningless little glyph that Dee Banton drew of the 'Templar Door' well over a year before I found it.

And of course I don't trust the inner beings one bit. Here's why, and read this carefully because it will transform your own inner life or throw you off the horse entirely...

***

I have no doubt that - up there/out there/in there - are what might be termed (though not by me) Higher Beings who exist in a different dimension. I have been aware of them all my life and can give you a million yarns as to their reality, without having any concrete ideas as to what they actually are. I've done an awful lot of work for them – every magician has – sometimes at great personal expense on numerous levels.

I've also known people under the impulse of very powerful levels of inner inspiration who have wanted to co-write books with me; who have tried to bully me with statements like: 'Give up your full time job and concentrate on our Work. The august being [N] is telling me this. [N] will make things right for you and your family. Trust and believe…'

Well bollocks to that. I never doubted the power or the reality of [N] in the psyches of my wanna-be co-writers but my response was always: 'If [N] wants me to do this work then it must send me a clear and unmistakeable sign by tea-time tomorrow. If [N] doesn't have the power to do that, then I'm not interested.'

[N] – and you have to visualise any one of six different Beings here – never did manage a sign.

To be fair to these people they all managed to get their projects off the ground eventually, sometimes years later, and did impressive jobs while finding out the hard way that books on magick don't make money.

Two things to bear in mind.

First, just because they're dead, doesn't mean They are wise.

Second, in Their other dimension, they don't have bills to pay. They don't get cold or hungry. They don't wake in the night worrying how They are going to cope, financially, in supporting their family. They don't have stressful jobs or horrible bosses or failing relationships. They don't experience the ultimate gut-churning agonies of having a very ill child. Even if They had ever been in incarnation and once knew these things, then in the timeless zones which They now inhabit, this would be all be forgotten, or minimised.

I learned long ago that the inner Beings have their own agenda, and can put inner pressures on us to do work in our realm without apparent concern for the difficulties we can experience here, in the Slough of Despond. Remember again: just because they're dead doesn't mean they're wise. I've known of 'Masters' who have given people, directly or directly, very poor advice when they're not churning out candy-floss philosophies.

You are not sheep. You can and should reproach Them and ask for practical support. Or simply tell Them to fuck off, as I have done often. ***Don't*** be meek and mild and say *Go away, oh please go away...* Give it some power and energy. It's the expression of intent and energy they understand. Be vulgar. You don't need a wand to do that.

Despite my intense dream about soldiers from another dimension I won't get into an excited lather about their imminent appearance.

* * *

Which brings me to another (ultimately relevant) yarn about a being called Ashtar.

I'd never heard of him, but sometime in 2002 I was being chuntered to by a woman in Chalice Orchard who had him as her guide. A pure and perfect being, she insisted, leader of some space fleet that was protecting us from aliens. Ashtar could tell her – and me – everything.

'Ask him to tell me why my bull-roarer won't work,' I responded, in all seriousness. (This device will become important later, so indulge me now.)

She babbled, she burbled. Or rather Ashtar did, through her. It was quite clear by then, even to her, that while Ashtar might be commanding fleets of spaceships across our galaxy, using all sorts of faster-then-light and inter-dimensional drives to traverse cosmic worm-holes, he hadn't a clue about my un-roaring piece of wood on a string.

I could see she was embarrassed.

'Sometimes,' she said, 'I wonder if Ashtar is just me talking to my higher self.'

Which was the whole thing about 'Philip' if you remember. I'll quote once more what Gray said to me as a very young man in my attempts to make inner contact with the Archangel Michael, because it is *crucial*:

> When you feel able to shut your eyes and 'call up' or 'evoke' a clear image of Michael in your mind – do so, and [see] what comes through. It will only answer you from the information you have 'banked' with yourself, *but* the way that information comes out and the new knowledge you gain from this should have come from the 'Michael-Concept' in our Cosmic, (or as Jung would have said: 'Collective') Consciousness.

And remember that he later added, when I had expressed some doubts about this:

> Yes, why didn't you try and make your Figures stand on their heads? Have a go at this, and when they refuse to obey silly or undignified suggestions, you'll know their 'Inners' are taking up the Images you obligingly made for them to occupy.

Now I'm not knocking Ashtar itself, because I know several people who use this image/interface to get very valid energies and information that do seem to come from outside themselves, as Carl Jung eventually experienced with his spirit guide Philemon.

Jung recounted a dream in which this figure first appeared to him. He saw an old man with kingfisher wings and the horns of a bull flying across the sky, carrying a bunch of keys. After the dream, he painted the image, because he did not understand it. During this intense period, Jung was struck by the synchronicity of finding a dead kingfisher, a bird rarely seen around Zürich, in his garden by the lakeshore. Thereafter Philemon, as he came to be named, played an important role in Jung's inner life. To Jung, he represented superior insight and functioned like a guru. In his memoirs he recounted that he would often converse with Philemon as he strolled in the garden of his lakeside home in Küsnacht, Switzerland. Speaking with Aniela Jaffé, his close friend and colleague, he recalled that:

> [Philemon] was simply a superior knowledge, and he taught me psychological objectivity and the actuality of the soul. He formulated and expressed everything which I had never thought.

At the moment, with the step-by-step creation of Ancuellos, I'll confess that I don't feel he is yet being energised and vivified to the extent that Philemon was, despite the innumerable small oddities that are happening in my outer world – too many to mention here. Perhaps my fellow-riders will have more success with him: regard Ancuellos as a coat of many colours that I've given you try on.

177

Amberaldus, on the other hand, seems at times to be *very* real.

***

I watched Harry and Meghan's wedding today. I'm sure that I could stretch out some magickal correspondences about this taking place in St George's Chapel, that saint being so important to the Templars. And that it took place in Windsor, in the Great Park of which the horned god Herne the Hunter has been seen and heard. But mainly I can remember in 1997 when I watched Harry as a small boy following his mother's coffin with his head bowed and the eyes of the world upon him. To see him today, with his gorgeous wife...

'You're having a hanky moment,' said Margaret, who has been known to watch the final scene of *ET* without misting up.

'Don't be ridiculous, Nobby...'

***

It was Lyn Picknett and Clive Prince who argued in *The Templar Revelation* that Jesus and Mary Magdalen, Simon Magus and Helen were exponents of a secret inner tradition of Sacred Sex that went back to Egyptian roots and the Mysteries of Isis and Osiris. And that their primary inspiration and even initiation into this came from John the Baptist, who was by no means the austere, insect-eating, desert-wandering solitary of popular imagination.

They go on to argue, I think successfully, that the 'John' tradition survived independently in the Middle East through the ancestors of the Mandaeans and the Nosairi. This was brought into Europe to join that of the

Magdalene, thus making sense of what might appear to have been separate male and female mysteries. They pointed out that the original nine Templar knights had emerged from Languedocian culture, the heart and soul of the Magdalene cult (and later on of the Cathars) – and that occult tradition has it that they learned their secrets 'from the Johannites of the East'.

It's not my place to expand upon this here, but if you do get their book read the later, revised edition, by which time they'd seen through the nonsense of the Priory of Sion and the whole tosh of Sacred Bloodlines. And ignore their obsession with Leonardo.

There are several other books whose theses dovetail quite neatly with the essence of this 'alternative history' and I'll mention these later in a bibliography so you can make you own mind up.

***

The whole concept of Sacred Marriage, and Marrying the Land was once fundamental to ancient cultures, which is why Ancuellos would have seen, felt and heard echoes of these amid the May festivities as he stood with his back to the door at Alton Priors. Some places seem to act as portals. I don't think it's so much that the 'veil is thin', but that – somehow - the liminality strips away all the outer layers of the mundane consciousness and the person standing in the doorway becomes part of this great interplay of heaven and earth, sun and soil, moon and water.

Perhaps the best writer to describe this was D.H. Lawrence in the very first page of his novel *The Rainbow.*

They felt the rush of the sap in spring, they knew the wave which cannot halt, but every year throws forward the seed to begetting, and, falling back, leaves the young-born on the earth. They knew the intercourse between heaven and earth, sunshine drawn into the breast and bowels, the rain sucked up in the daytime, nakedness that comes under the wind in autumn, showing the birds' nests no longer worth hiding. Their life and interrelations were such; feeling the pulse and body of the soil, that opened to their furrow for the grain, and became smooth and supple after their ploughing, and clung to their feet with a weight that pulled like desire, lying hard and unresponsive when the crops were to be shorn away. The young corn waved and was silken, and the lustre slid along the limbs of the men who saw it. They took the udder of the cows, the cows yielded milk and pulse against the hands of the men, the pulse of the blood of the teats of the cows beat into the pulse of the hands of the men. They mounted their horses, and held life between the grip of their knees, they harnessed their horses at the wagon, and, with hand on the bridle-rings, drew the heaving of the horses after their will.

There were certainly times when, sitting in a vast and empty field below the Salisbury Plain I've felt a complete connectedness which I made my character Kaspar O'Malley describe in detail in my novel *Twisted Light*. But I suppose I should yarn now about old 'Dirty Bertie' as he was once known, as it's relevant to how we might deal with any inner beings that we might summon, stir and call up into our dreams.

When I was a young man I was obsessed by David Herbert Lawrence (1885-1930). The parallels between his life, as expressed in *Sons and Lovers* and my own growing up in an identical mining background, seemed uncanny. I read everything about his life that I could find and adored the title of one biography by Harry T. Moore: *Priest of Love*. At one point I think I could have gone on Mastermind answering questions about him. Being young and daft I made the assumption that I *must* be a reincarnation, although I didn't tell anyone that, thank goodness. But I was constantly on the lookout for my own Jessie Chambers, Louie Burrows, Alice Dax (who took him upstairs and 'gave him sex'), and Frieda von Richtofen, in an unconscious attempt to create my own saga of group return, even though I had not become aware of this concept at that early age.

The problem was, when I came to write my own fiction I was swamped by sub-Lawrencian turgidity to the extent that I couldn't tell a simple yarn. Everyone's bloods were always flowing together and warmed by dark fires. Eventually I wrote a comic novel called *Shimmying Hips* in which every aspect was a mickey-take of Bert. I think only three people have ever read it, but at least I got him out of my system and I was able to find my own voice. I don't expect anyone to buy that one. I'm not sure how Marcia  Pickands (and many others) managed this with respect to Dion Fortune but they will have gone through the same sort of foggy glamour.

The moral here, as I've said before, is that we all get a little bit daft, and think daft things. If anyone reading this has similar perturbations going on now then don't worry about it. Just don't inflict anything on others, and get ready to jettison *everything* even if you feel driven by the Ashtar Command, the Great White Brotherhood or the innermost Order of the Poor Knights.

***

So much writing about the Knights Templar is often tied in with the Holy Grail, in which I've got no interest. That raises eyebrows because in the Western Traditions, aspiration toward this is almost compulsory. Just as I've no interest in the Holy Land, and no interest in Jesus except as an ordinary fella, I don't know and don't really care what the Grail might have been, whether it's a chalice, severed head or bloodline. Believe me, I've read all the books. At the end of this one I'll include an old essay I did years ago which marked my severance from the Grail's tyranny in my own youth at least and show that there must always – *always* – be Another Way.

The fact is, I'm only interested in my Wiltshire Templars and what they might have absorbed. I don't care about the richly documented Templars in neighbouring Somerset. When I was writing bits and pieces in my little garden office this morning the pc went insane. I won't blame the Windows 10 updates for that one. Getting somewhat tetchy, I thought I'd better not use the grand English expression and tell the Templars to stop 'buggering' about in case they misunderstood, so I said instead: *Look lads, I'm doing something that is actually on your behalf.* **Stop** *it!*

The computer then behaved itself instantly.

Chapter 14

White Horses and their ilk

The original plan for today was another attempt at a picnic on Knap Hill. In the event we decided that a) it would still be crowded with paragliders b) it was too hot to walk anywhere. So we had our picnic in the shed at the bottom of our garden, among the faeries. It's odd but the garden behind immediately ours belongs to a man in the next street who was initiated into the Society of the Inner Light years ago. I'm not a member of that august group but in some ways it is my spiritual home. Although a former reverend, he has a vast collection of books on magick. We meet up at irregular intervals and have puddings at the excellent café in Trowbridge Library and talk about...well, nothing deep. If I ever do this book about searching for the White Christ I might ask him to co-write, even though I've found this sort of thing problematic in the past.

I don't really want to talk much about Templars as such today, as I think the White Horses of Wiltshire might want a yarn or two flung in their direction.

In fact horses were a definite Templar obsession. They were an absolutely essential part of a knight's equipment. You needed four powerful warhorses known as destriers. They were as vital to Age of Chivalry as tanks were in the Second World War: whoever had the most and/or most powerful tanks would always win. They were trained to endure the noise and horror and smell of battle. They were also trained, in later years, to lash out at enemies with teeth and hooves thereby becoming, a *weapon* as well as a fighting platform. They rode stallions, not mares or geldings, because they were thought to be more aggressive.

Being human, all too human, these horses (and knights had to have four) were a status thing, every bit as much as having a Porsche or Ferrari is today. Or, if you're not quite in the top bracket, an Audi – which seemingly empowers you to tailgate anyone on the narrow roads of Wiltshire.

Wiltshire has a curious obsession with white horses, although none of them are as ancient as the dragon-like beast at Uffington. There are eight surviving examples  and folk-memories of numerous others. The one that concerns me and Margaret is the Westbury White Horse which is scoured into the northernmost edge of Salisbury Plain and can be seen from the end of our street. There is a winding road to the top and large area to park and you can stand on its extreme slope if you've got the nerve. I haven't.

The one that exists today is only a few hundred years old and faces east. But there seems to have been a much older one facing west. This one was beak nosed, short legged  with a marked crescent on the tip of its serpent-like tail, moons and crescents on its saddlecloth, with single cyclopean eye. Locals called it affectionately the moon-stallion. Pegasus this is not, but I'll wager that any good shaman could get this beast to fly.

In fact there are numerous folk tales about the various Wiltshire steeds coming alive. Because I'm running out of steam today forgive me while I quote my own self from *Spirits of the Stones*:

> Although the White Horses of Wiltshire were undoubtedly linked with the horse-cults among the tribes who lived there, it may well be that something else was involved also. Of course, it is not always wise to look for neat explanations of things that find expression on magickal levels. Sometimes it is best to let Mystery prevail. One common exclamation among occultists is that if they had wanted to make their experiences up, they would have described events which were far more explicable than those which had so bewildered them

Recent findings in Peru of huge anthropomorphic figures echoing the famed Nazca 'lines' have been defined rather neatly as 'geoglyphs'. They are felt to represent supernatural beings or, more likely, shamans, and were created perhaps between the years AD 200-700. Most of the White Horses in Wiltshire are relatively modern geoglyphs, no more than 300 or 400 years old with the one at Alton Barnes considerably younger than that. Yet I like to think that the locals felt compelled to create these as – perhaps - stylised representations of what might be called their spirit 'allies', to hijack a shamanic concept and term. That's another thing that Bill Gray told me: that the country folk had their own awareness of things going on below the surface, but they don't talk about it. He emphasised those last six words individually, perhaps to make it sink into my teenage brain. They did.

Certainly folk-tales around Alton Barnes concern a mysterious white horse being seen at the dew ponds on certain occasions such as dawn or on moonlit nights. I think they can be used as keys to unlock the hidden door within the psyche of the individual and give access to the indwelling spirit of the land around. This, I feel, will segue into the fascinating topic of Crop Circles before too long, but at the moment I need to rest after having had cameras up my arse and things cut out of me while the nurses around spoke of nothing else but Harry and Meghan and how happy they all were.

Really, it was an odd occasion and fertile ground for many jokes, most of them relating to the times I've had my head up my arse. This time, as the surgeon navigated his camera through my darkest depths, I was able to watch it all on a large screen. 'There are three things I need to cut out,' he said, 'in case they turn malign and give you trouble later.'

Given my earlier injunction that every reader should look at everything happens as a 'secret dealing' etc etc, then how can I interpret those three 'things' lurking within me? School bullies? Treacherous old flames? No that's quite simple now: I've given them the names of the Father, Son and Holy Ghost and will be glad to get rid of them at the last.

Margaret was waiting for me when I came out of surgery.

'Last week you had the Templar Head giving you gyp, now it's the Templar Arse,' she observed.

I couldn't think of anything witty to say. After 36 hours of no food and dreadful liquids to make me crap, I was desperate for a Kitkat…

On a lighter note:

It has always been a mild delight to me that the outline of the county of Wiltshire seems to be that of a spiky-haired man looked westward.

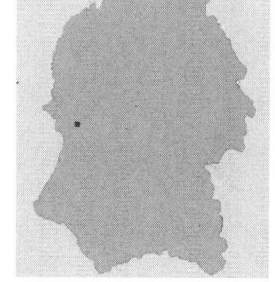

'Margarete, mon amour, avez-vous noticed that the outline matches my profile exactly? Wiltshire is a Head and the Head is *moi*. I must be the very incarnation of the dark fires which underlie the county.'

'Bollocks,' she said.

I've noticed that she uses this word a lot in response to many of my statements. I might have to tell her that because I'm a mighty Adept they're actually Annunciations, to be taken seriously and without question.

'And where we live is actually at the place of the *ajna chakra*, to which I've brought you after coming on my white horse to find you in Gomorrah. I think in future you should call me 'Mr. Wiltshire', or simply 'Wiltshire', as a manifestation of this county and all the bloods that flow within it.'

'Double bollocks. You were born and raised in Northumberland, you eejit. But I'll call you Mr. Wilt if you insist.'

'Actually, it doesn't look like me at all...'

***

It was while I was recovering from that minor piece of surgery yesterday that I felt compelled to contact Jacobus Swart, whom Bill Gray regarded as his Magical Son and whose insight into the Kabbalah is several hundred years beyond mine. These days as I more and more 'wither into the root', to use a Yeatsian term, I find the mighty all-embracing Tree of Life with its myriad branches too much. I'm happy to stay in the crack of that old yew tree at Alton Priors that Ancuellos would have known, sucking up the energies from what lies beneath. But Jacobus is a genius in his tradition and anyone who contacts him won't have to pay for litres of kabbalah water. Madonna could have saved herself a fortune if she'd found him first.

Jacobus and I fell out some years ago. I can't remember what about now. It was probably me being a complete pillock as I'm wont to be at frequent intervals. For readers from overseas who arc unfamiliar with this term it is a word of mid-16th Century origin, a variant of the archaic word pillicock, meaning 'penis'. I suppose it is better than being thought of as a cunt, as I fear I've also sometimes been at exquisitely embarrassing times in the past.

Maybe, as Margaret says, I do have to become my own Grand Master and forgive myself. I know it won't help me asking that young lad Jesus.

In fact William G. Gray fell out with *everyone* but he was not alone in that. The Western Mystery Tradition seems to produce spiky and often touchy individuals. I think it was Naomi Ozaniec (who knows her stuff) who coined the delicious phrase Western Misery Tradition. Mind you, don't let the pagans in their covens fool you into thinking they're all warm and loving, saying Merry Meet, or Merry Part and Go Well, and giving big hugs and glugging cider while making corn dollies. They are perhaps more touchy about initiations and successions and who is or isn't the 'true' inheritor of things than anyone. The only thing I regret about not belonging to any of those groups is that I don't hear the gossip.

At a certain age you (I) realise with horror that life is short and sometimes fierce. Many of my yarns about individuals now begin with the phrase: 'The late…' which brings me up with a shock. So I took a deep breath and – probably prodded by the Great Beast of Cheltenham himself - made contact with Jacobus again. We're both delighted, even though we'll never meet.

When I started this Templar 101 I didn't expect Bill Gray to keep popping up in the way he has. It has made me think: Was the Templar that Ray saw standing next to me an aspect of Gray? I have a fairly formidable memory of my meetings with him (not to mention a box of still unpublished letters) and I am certain he never once mentioned the 'T' word. Our concerns were very much about Dion Fortune, the energies of the land, the – to him – spurious nature of the term 'wicca', which he loathed, even though he worked High Magic with enough of the early witches. But Templars were never mentioned.

With Jacobus, however, Bill expounded upon them at length. To give you a brief overview of Jacobus' email you need to know a bit about Papus first…

Papus was the pseudonym of the Spanish-born French physician Dr. Gérard Encausse (1865-1916). He is to the magical traditions of Europe what William Marshal was to the Age of Chivalry.

At the age of 26, Encausse claimed to have come into the possession of the original papers of Martinez Paschalis, and therewith founded an Order of Martinists called *l'Ordre des Supérieurs Inconnus*.

At the age of 28 he was consecrated a bishop of *l'Église Gnostique de France* by Jules Doinel, who had founded this Church as an attempt to revive the Cathar religion. In 1895, Doinel abdicated as Primate of the French Gnostic Church, leaving control of the Church to a synod of three of his former bishops, one of whom was Encausse.

Among many other magical Orders he was also X° of the *Ordo Templi Orientis*, and established the 'Supreme Grand Council General of the Unified Rites of Ancient and Primitive Masonry for the Grand Orient of France and its Dependencies at Paris.'

That is the briefest of summaries. You don't need to know much about any of these arcane organisations and I personally no longer have any interest in them. Basically he was a figure of enormous importance and influence in the occult world and who died aged 51 while serving at the front in the Great War.

In short, beneath all the titles and the esoteric glamour, he was the real thing.

And then there was...

Emile Napoleon Hauenstein who was young Bill Gray's Austrian mentor, a Martinist who worked with Papus. Bill's extraordinary American mum, (née Christine Chester Logie), was quite certain that ENH, as he was always called, was a reincarnation of Eliphas Levi. She thoroughly approved of their relationship. If you want more details then you can track down *The Old Sod*, the biography that Marcus Claridge and I wrote about all these people and their times.

So this is what Jacobus said about Bill and the Templars...

From what I understood of the Theoclet/Templar saga as related by Bill, is that Papus (Gerard

Encause) told E.N.H. when he passed the 'Rod' to him, that the masonic story and Eliphas Levi's retelling of this saga, was inaccurate. He maintained that Theoclet, who was apparently the leader of the Johannites, a sect who revered John the Baptist, were not on friendly terms with Hugues de Payens at all. In fact, he stated that this first grandmaster of the Templars and his companions attacked the Johannites whom they branded heretics, and that as Hugues de Payens was slaying Theoclet, the latter individual held a stick (the Rod) up into the face of Hugues de Payens, who snatched it with contempt as he slayed Theoclet with his sword. On grabbing the 'stick' (Rod), Payens was overwhelmed with the power of the Rod, which I can go into if you want to hear it, and which I can attest to, but which I am loath to discuss because nobody will believe it, and it is really not of the slightest importance whether anyone believe it or not anyway. Be that as it may, the end of the saga is that Hugues de Payens was apparently overcome with remorse, and tried to save the life of Theoclet who succumbed to his injuries. I have tried my damndest over the years to find further details on this saga, and have not succeeded to find anything more than unsubstantiated hints here and there, but nothing to write home about. Anyway, according to what E.N.H. told Bill, that is the way Hugh de Payens became the second carrier of the 'Rod', and after that it was passed on amongst the Templars from one grandmaster to the next.

This is all new to me. And then he came out with a real gem that compensated for my not being able to access the Temple Church in Bristol that day:

It would seem there were some very interesting discoveries made near Bristol while excavating the foundations of an original Templar Church. It involved an upright altar, Eastern Orthodox style, such as is used in many Western Inner Tradition temples and lodges. In this instance there was an opening (aumbry?) in the said altar, inside which was kept a chalice or vessel which held a few drops of blood from every member of that 'Commanderie'. Ostensibly this was so that, whether they were sent to the Holy Land or not, they could all claim that they had shed blood for the 'cause', and there was the blood to prove it. According to Bill that was the 'Sangreal' in practical symbology. Naturally I was very interested to hear that, but I am not sure whether this was general Templar practice or not, since very little is known about the ceremonies of that Order which was kept secret.

Hmmm…and then:

…fundamentally the saga of the Templars for Bill, and perforce myself as an individual to whom he passed his 'Rod', was the sort of 'lineage of the Rod,' i.e. how it commenced with Theoclet from whence it was passed to Hugues de Payens, and then along the list of grandmasters until the arrest of Jacques de Molay, when it left France and ended up in Scotland, and from thence back to Baron von Hund, the founder of the Masonic 'Rite of Strict Observance,' and ever onward to a variety of individuals like Martinez de Pasqualis, Henri Delaage, Antoine Chaptal, Papus, and so forth. How true any of this is I cannot say, because Bill never quoted references, neither in his writings nor in his speech. He simply related what he knew, believed it to be correct, and conjectured freely about the rest. Bill saw the connection between all these individuals, ourselves included, as a 'Line of Light' running through all of us.

All of this came out of the blue but I won't follow it up. I know that at least a few of my readers will find their nape hairs prickling with excitement about certain things in that email so I think it is time you find your own destrier, ride your own path toward Jacobus if you want, and leave me to trot along by myself now.

And if you have to ask me how to find him, then you're not showing much imagination at all...

Chapter 15

Sovereignty …

We're an odd match, me and the Templars. I'm not an academic, yet they seem to need one to expand upon their Mysteries. Sorry lads but I can't do that! I'm clever, or so I'm told, but I'm not a scholar. And nor am I an Alpha Male, as you'd expect all Templar Knights to be, so it's not as if they can see anything in common there. I've written at length elsewhere about that chthonic character in my life Maxwell, who helpfully points out that on the toughest, roughest manliest time in my teens I was never even a Beta Male and spent most of those years whingeing and whining at the levels of Gamma and Delta Males.

It strikes me as I write this, that if I *did* have an incarnation in Templar times, then I'd have been the treacherous little shit who would have betrayed them to the authorities for my 30 pieces of silver. Perhaps that is why I'm doing this? Redemption? Atonement? Then again I'm fully aware of my tendency to tell stories, especially to myself. This wouldn't be a case of 'far memory' but of far-fetched myth-making. It would make a good yarn but I won't be wearing any hair-shirts.

***

When I wrote those bits in the last chapter about Papus and ENH it felt like wading through mud – and you know my feelings about that substance. I'm not even sure they would approve of (or even understand) my own inner direction. My passion is for the silent and subtle Earth Mysteries whereas theirs is all to do with blood and guts and severed heads and a Holy Land which is as holy and helpful to me as the Inquisition was to them. I'll do my best to honour the *Wiltshire* Templars but I've no interest in a bigger picture and I'm not sure that the construct of Ancuellos is helping me clarify things.

Perhaps this relates to the ridiculous dream that I had last night. There was a group of us, complete strangers, who were involved a competition for a big prize. The contest would be won by whichever person was able to slice a chunk of ham the thinnest! Some of my rivals used sophisticated cutting machines. I was determined to get my slice thin enough to be held up to the window like stained glass, and I'd only use a knife.

Well that's truly a stupid dream, but on reflection while sitting here in Trowbridge library again, I suppose it's what I've been doing with the huge chunk of 'Templar meat' that I started with: cutting it down to its absolutely thinnest slice.

I was quite troubled this morning when I woke up. Not because of the dream imagery itself but because I'm feeling that in various ways this whole project is being hi-jacked by the energy or entity we might think of as 'William G. Gray'. I've no doubt that someone reading this might be tempted to send me a message from the spirit of Gray but don't bother unless you know the code word we agreed upon before his death. He was quite adamant that he was going to reincarnate – and quickly – in America and so any such messages would be – in his words – pure crap. So far, no-one has given me the code word which would verify any such contact. Please save your messages for yourself.

I do get a sense that 'Amberaldus' is an actual and formidable energy on the inner planes and I'm trying not to conflate him/it with Gray. In fact I'll do the 'trying and testing of the spirits' that was a feature of medieval magick to see whether they 'cut the mustard' to use an old-fashioned term. Mustard, thinly sliced ham…there's a metaphor in there somewhere. So I'm going to challenge Ameraldus now, and as the wireless network here in the library is going haywire again I'll send out my inner signal before it all crashes.

> *If there are any Templar revenants lurking around on the inner planes, I want a clear and unmistakeable signal in my life by 5 pm today. If it doesn't arrive then I'm going to go happily trotting along in my own way, in my own direction, and if you want to learn anything from this then you can. Otherwise…*

This challenge might seem crass but it will become relevant very soon.

I feel a bit better now.

***

Well, I had a huge afternoon nap after that. Nearly three hours of dreamless sleep that made up for the previous broken nights. I felt terrific. Nothing appeared in my life in any shape or form that might have significance.

On another level for her own reasons, Margaret was deeply troubled by issues of her own so I created a simple visualisation of us both being on the white horse, in our crude armours as described earlier. We dismounted, removed the helmets so that we could see the world and its affects properly instead of through a narrow slot, removed the heavy protective metals which covered our trunk and legs, then simply and lightly clad we walked together toward a glade that has always held magick for us.

There was more to it than that, and done more artfully than I sketch here, but the feeling afterward was one of renewal.

***

One of the underlying themes of this book has been that of the Sacred Marriage and consciousness of the Land. It has not always blended easily or obviously with the Templar themes and, like a frisky horse, I've often had to jerk the reins to head in my direction and not theirs.

There was a time when, in 2004, we stood atop of Westbury White Horse and decided that all we saw before us was 'our' kingdom, to which we would assume a degree of responsibility and involvement. When travelling beyond this small realm of West Wiltshire we would ask the indwelling spirits of the land for entry and safe passage. When we re-enter we give our personal Great Incantation. Only two people have ever heard this: Jo Clark in the sycamore grove where we lived, and David Walker, the book boy of Glastonbury, in the grounds of the Bishop's Palace in Wells. Both of them were deeply shaken by the experience.

That all sounds very clunky and probably pretentious writing it like that, but the reality was/is silent and simple and has reaped benefits over the years.

(Everyone, I would add, no matter where they live, should do the same. Just don't go around telling everyone that you're now the King or Queen of Chicken Leg, Ohio, because no-one will go for it and that's not how it works anyway. As Eliphas Levi said: you must *Know, Will, Dare – and above all be Silent.* And he was right.)

As Sharon Blackie wrote, the native pre-Christian mythology of the Celtic nations is highly woman-centred. In the oldest stories, the creative, generative essence of the universe was female, not male; women represented the spiritual and moral axis of the world, and the power of men was predominantly social.

> But the Celtic divine female was a long way from the remote, transcendent sky-deities we've grown used to in recent centuries here in the West: she had one foot in the Otherworld for sure, but she was firmly grounded and deeply rooted in place, indivisible from her distinctive, haunting landscapes. In Ireland in particular, the Dinnseanchas - the ancient stories and lore of place, the foundation-stones both of personal and communal identity, and of moral obligations to the land and the tribe - tell us how so many major features of the landscape came to be named after women... Ancient Irish literature is filled with stories of powerful women who were incarnations of Sovereignty, the goddess of the land who was its guardian and protector. Sovereignty was the spirit of the Earth itself, the anima mundi, a deeply ecological force.[3]

I think that we're in realms here that cannot easily be explained yet which can be worked toward and attained by all. Over the years we have empowered (or rather gained power from) impressive and often isolated trees in our area by giving them names. The concept of the *ren* here again. In J.D. Wakefield's book that I plundered in an earlier chapter he names the ancient goddess as Anna and also regards the complex of hills beyond Alton Priors as a manifestation of Gwenevere.

Molly Larkin, writing on the same theme, referred to the ceremony in ancient Ireland in which the kind would marry the land, or more accurately marry the Goddess of the land. This marriage meant that the King swore to protect the land and the people, and be a caretaker of the earth. This ceremony, which continued well into the 16th Century, would take place during the Celtic celebration of Beltane, the 1st of May, which is a time of fertility and new beginnings. Whatever simple steps you might take to recognise the spirit of Earth will be acts of High Magick in the long run.

Molly goes on to list things which we can all *do* without needing to invoke dubious inner beings:

'Make a commitment to be a caretaker of the earth, to marry the land. Here are some ways to do it:

- **Recycle** always
- Bring re-usable **shopping bags** to the grocery store – always
- Carry a refillable water bottle instead of buying individual pre-packaged water bottles
- Offer corn meal or tobacco as a **blessing/offering to the earth** on a regular basis
- **Pick up litter**, regardless of whether or not it's yours
- Think about your impact in all of your actions
- Think ahead **7 generations**
- Instead of seeding a water-guzzling lawn, plant a **wildflower meadow**
- **Support** environmental organizations
- **Plant** trees
- Buy **local** food
- Turn off lights and **unplug** appliances when they're not in use
- Pay bills online to **save paper**

- **Bless the land**, bless the trees
- Write/call your Congressional representative demanding they **take action on environmental causes** and climate change. Remind them of their sacred duty to protect the people and the earth on which we live.
- Better yet, vote for political leaders who will make such a commitment to caring for the land.

Such commitments can be the equivalent of marrying the land, honoring and caretaking her. And we will all be better off for it.'

Molly's suggestions were already natural to both of us, although I'm probably Virtue Signalling here, which I loathe in anyone else. They probably arose after that first time standing atop of Westbury White Horse and making our commitment both to each other and to our immediate realm. But we did have one experience up there, in the pitch dark, which had nothing to do with the Land and – seemingly – everything to do with the Stars.

Forget riding behind me on the horse. Forget the bloody Templars for a moment. The next bit might seem to take us VERY far from the egregore of the Order of Poor Knights but bear with me. We will soon find ourselves at Alton Priors again, with our backs to the Templar Door and looking north toward the White Horse of Alton Barnes.

Walk alongside while I now give you the *weirdest* of yarns…

***

It all starts with the bull-roarer. I first saw this lump of wood on a string in the small shop of a small fort in

Kentucky in 1975. I've forgotten the name of the place but it looked exactly like all those I've seen in Westerns over my lifetime. I asked the young man behind the counter what this thing was, and why would anyone possibly want one. He took it outside, unfurled the string, whizzed it around his head and the noise it made was wonderful.

'That'll be $5, buddy.'

'No thanks,' I replied. As I was selling my plasma at the time for $10 a pint just to survive, that was bit too much.

The second time I saw/heard a bullroarer was on the film *Crocodile Dundee II* when he took one out of his pocket and whizzed it to see if, in my half-remembered words, anyone was around...

I tried to make one but it was useless, as I said earlier. Then Margaret bought me a proper device and I couldn't wait to try it out.

Which is why we found ourselves in pitch darkness on the top of Westbury White Horse, standing on top of the Long Barrow there and me whirling it as hard as I could. To be honest, with the slight breeze and my rotten lugholes, I couldn't hear a damned thing, but I felt it was doing *something* to the aethyrs, though I couldn't tell what.

Instead of ancient, half-forgotten gods and goddesses or ancestral wraiths a massive UFO appeared behind the thin clouds instead, large as a couple of football fields and lights on the bottom in a rough M shape. From my teenage days in the Air Training Corps I was irritatingly expert in aircraft recognition. This was not earthly.

I have to say that Margaret panicked. I wanted to signal it with my flashlight and get beamed up to have group sex with comely Etherian ladies from a parallel dimension. Instead she begged me to get in the car and drive – fast! – away from there. I'm famous for not driving fast but I did manage at least 25 mph on the road down the hill.

I still think we missed something that night.

Everyone's UFO stories get boring very quickly. I did see one when I was 15 and walking through the night in Keilder Forest, Northumberland, on a school trip. No need to say any more than that.

I'm encouraged to even mention the above two incidents without embarrassment because of Canon Anthony Duncan. Listen everyone, forget Baphomet, Huges de Payens and Jacques de Molay, put aside Papus, ENH, WGG and that phoney AR. Tony Duncan had more light about him than anyone and I don't care if he believed profoundly in that fella Jesus.

***

Anthony Duncan (1930-2003), the son of a Scots father and an English mother, joined the army and served in Germany and the Far East until resigning his commission as a thirty-year-old captain in order to follow his spiritual calling. Upon his return to civilian life he entered Chichester Theological College and was ordained into the Anglican church, first serving as a curate and later as parish priest to five parishes in both Gloucestershire and Northumberland. During that time he was also made an honorary Canon of Newcastle Cathedral.

Profoundly psychic individuals I know were all in awe of Duncan's own talents and for a time he was a 'release worker' for the Church of England. That is to say, an exorcist; although you're not supposed to say that out

 loudly. C. of E. though he may have been, but he was also capable of having benign communications with Pan, see the living faces within the rocks of the Allen Valley, negotiate with faery beings when he accidentally disrupted their realm, talk to the old stones of Northumberland and – the clincher for me – a keen aeromodeller. His books include *The Tao of Christ: A Christian's Reading of the Daodejing of Laozi; The Way of Transcendence; Temple of the Spirit; Celtic Christianity* (a favourite of mine)*; The Sword in the Sun: Dialogue with an Angel; A Little Book of Celtic Prayer;* and his most well-known work – *Christ, Psychotherapy and Magic.*

Gareth Knight goes into more detail about him in his esoteric autobiography, *I called it Magic*, and also *Christ and Qabalah.*[5]

I spoke to him on the phone a couple of times, mainly about our mutual Northumbrian links, but we never met. That is another regret of mine. I'm sure he could have resolved some of the dilemmas I've always had with respect to this notion of 'Christ'. (And please please please… I don't want any readers of this to email me with their own solutions. I will ignore them all.) Duncan's concern was with the old Celtic saints who were almost precursors of the Cathars - working human beings with dirt under their nails, peaceful and ascetic wanderers who tried to enhance the quality of life for themselves and their people. He also wrote at length on reincarnation, psychism, the 'universal feminine principle' and how the legacy of St Augustine has served to replace the latter with a malignant misogyny.

I could probably fall in love with a man like that.

But with respect to beings from other worlds he also wrote the very curious book *To Think Without Fear*, subtitled *The Challenge of the Extra-Terrestrial*.[6] In it he does seem to bend over backward, in ways I don't wholly follow, to reconcile this challenge of extra-terrestrials who have never heard of Jesus with his own very profound belief in that fella. In the chapter entitled 'A Mutual Attempt At Communication' he begins:

> Since our arrival in Corbridge, and particularly during the months November and December 1995, and at intervals afterward, we have been visited by what I have come to understand as no less than four different groups of non-terrestrial persons.

In simple schoolboy-ish terms I allow myself to think: if Anthony Duncan says this, it *must* be true. He even goes on to describe the differing types, beginning with the first group of tall, solemn beings he encountered previously at Whitley Mill who were from a different Universe altogether. And then gives a summary of the other groups, in terms of character and appearance. While he struck up an affectionate bond with the 'leader' of one of them, whom for sake of fun he called 'Jimmy', another group was inclined to regard us a 'species' to be investigated. He added:

> It has been necessary to make it clear to this group that I will be treated by them on equal terms or not at all! This caused them evident consternation and they have not returned since.

Which, as I've already shown, is an attitude to take toward ALL the inner beings whether from Cygnus or Lusignan.

The fourth group he found was altogether more primitive and had to be firmly but kindly told to leave – albeit with his blessing!

> I am inclined to think that technology of some kind may be involved in the appearance here of some or all of these groups, and this might have a bearing on the many, and differing accounts of UFOs and their alleged inhabitants. But this is speculation on my part, I do not know.

I've known mystics and magicians sneer at the very idea of ETs while developing inner contacts with the most extraordinary range of inner beings. In the light of Duncan's experiences, given the absolute integrity of the man, I do think they are missing out.

***

Because I've always had this freakish ability to believe and disbelieve at the same time without losing my equilibrium, I've read all the books about extra-terrestrial Contacts. I read them as voraciously as Margaret reads Thrillers, both of us finding a sort of light relief in our respective genres but neither of us taking them as life-enhancing. Although I give books away as quickly as I get them, Timothy Good's: *Earth – an Alien Enterprise* is one that I will keep and read again and again, at long intervals. I love it for the yarns! It makes me go *Hmmm...* more than any other.

Two little nuggets from this will get us back to Alton Priors and the Templar Door.

Good gives several stories which suggest that extra-terrestrials are actually living among us now, largely unrecognised, and going about their own business without any fuss – one of them even working as a shelf-stacker in a supermarket. Dee Banton confirms this from her own experience and David Conway in his autobiography *Magic without Mirrors* describes his relationship with one in Brussels, one Hubert Wattiaux, before the latter's untimely death. In my own varied working life with vulnerable and supposedly disturbed people I've met a few individuals who… well, I'd better leave it at that for now. Suffice to say:

They exist. They're here. Make sure we all treat each other as equals.

***

In February 1967 Timothy Good was playing with the London Symphony Orchestra in New York for a series of concerts at Carnegie Hall with Mstislav Rostropovich, the great Russian cellist. He decided to try and initiate a contact telepathically with extra-terrestrials living among us. So, on that late afternoon, between a rehearsal and concert, he sat down in the lobby of the Park-Sheraton Hotel at 56th Street on Seventh Avenue and transmitted a telepathic request: 'If any of you people from elsewhere are in the New York vicinity, please come and sit down right next to me and prove it.'

> After about half an hour a man entered the lobby whose demeanour put me on the alert. Dressed in a charcoal-gray suit with a white shirt and dark tie, he could have passed for a businessman from Madison Avenue. He wore rimmed glasses and appeared to be about thirty-five years old and five feet ten inches in height, with slightly curly fair hair, a mild olive complexion, and perfectly proportioned features. He sat down beside me,

took out a copy of The New York Times from his attaché case, and turned the pages over in a rather deliberate and superficial manner. After he had refolded the paper, I asked him telepathically if he really was from another planet, and if so, to please confirm this by placing his right index finger on the right side of his nose and - I vaguely recall -asking him to keep it there for a short while. No sooner had I transmitted the thought than he did precisely that.

Although Good attempted more telepathy no further confirmation was forth-coming. Eventually the man stood up, walked over to some display windows and then gave him a direct and serious look before walking out of the hotel into Seventh Avenue never to be seen again. Good concluded: 'I am often asked why I didn't try and engage him in a conversation, to which I can only respond that it seemed inappropriate. I assumed that, if conversation was to be on the agenda, he would be the one to initiate it.'

***

Inspired by these yarns and also a sense of whimsy I did the same as Timothy Good. I sent out a signal to any aliens out there and invited them to make contact with me the next day. To be completely honest I then forgot all about doing this. It was only in the afternoon when I was emerging heavily-laden from Poundland in the Shires shopping centre that I was pushed rather fiercely in the back by someone. The man was 30-ish, had immaculately groomed silvery-blonde hair and piercing blue eyes. He simply said *Hello*, then turned and walked off.

Coincidence? I prefer to act 'as if' and suspend disbelief because that adds so much more to the wonder of life. If I see him again I'll…I'll… actually I don't know what I'll do or say! Probably just leave him alone. Also, I must confess that he looked uncannily like a short-haired version of some of the illustrations of Ashtar that you can find on-line, but not the ones with the stupid helmet.

Make of that what you want.

***

Of course, extra-terrestrials and faeries are the sort of topics that can suck you into their vortices, as I've got a dozen other tales that are struggling to be heard. I simply include this particular yarn to show you where I got the idea of challenging the inner Templars to send me a clear and unmistakeable Sign. No such Sign appeared, on any level, either because they've gone, or never existed outside of my imagination, or they're just a kind of astral shell and don't have the power these days. Somewhere in all that I hope at least a couple of my readers will find ways to be as whimsical with their own inner stuff.

And now, because I'm a bit under the weather with all these energies flitting back and forth, I really do want us to get back to Alton Priors again, where I feel pure…

Chapter 16

Circles and their Crops

Bit of a disaster this morning. I woke with a vague sense of unease but put it down to sinusitis, Templar Head-and-Arse aches, plus various other low-grade anxieties. In fact some of the water pipes in the kitchen had been happily gurgling their leaks overnight and I think it was the *lares*, the Spirit of our House (for whom we have a *ren* and image) who was trying to alert me. For her part Margaret found that her laptop wasn't connecting and doing various bizarre but low-grade things.

'It's your fucking Templars again,' she ventured.

Because of my magnificent ineptitude for anything DIY (something I inherited from my Dad) I'm completely covered by all sorts of policies that will summon help in an emergency, up to but not including thermo-nuclear explosions. In due course a nice plumber phoned from Gloucester and said he'd be down in a few hours. When he arrived, he gave a low whistle and pointed out that the fault lay in our stopcock. I don't know what the American term is, but this is the device which controls all the water coming from the mains into our system.

'Look at *that!*' he marvelled, holding the (not old) errant piece up to show me. I didn't know what I was looking at and didn't care, as long the new one worked and didn't leak. Then he added: 'Wow, I've never seen anything like *that* before…'

I'm sure that in the context of this project the bizarre failure of my stopcock must be deeply symbolic, and Dr Jung would have been in ecstasies. If truth be told to power, then I'm rather wearied with the Order of the

Poor Knights and also the way that Bill Gray keeps popping up. I suspect that some of my readers are too. These beings/energies/entities fantasies or earthbound spirits don't seem to move on. Speculations about to their Mysteries fall into the category (for me at least) of 'same old same old'.

I suppose I'm happiest standing with my back to the Templar Door that I first discovered in the days of rising sap when this book was started and felt that it might be a useful interface.

Interface between what?

I mentioned much earlier about the False Doors that were features on some Egyptian tombs. These were built into all tombs from the 2nd Dynasty onward. They were never meant to be opened in the physical sense. The idea was that if there was an appropriate sense of connection between the observer and the departed, then the *ka* of the latter would appear within the frame like a picture on a computer screen today. With a respect to a particular being/energy/entity named Kha'm-uast, I once wrote:

> To those who have been brought up in the television age the time of the 'false door' has come around again. The Traveller can use any clear space of wall to create his screen, in lieu of an actual temple. In Kha'm-uast's case the originally blank stone was tuned into his frequency and his alone, by means of hieroglyphic statements.

However, with respect to our Templar Door, there is no sense that in its heyday it was created with this sort of interface in mind. When the church was built it would have been solid oak with all sort of carvings and fiddly iron-work to make it look like the Priest's Door in Orchardleigh. I'm inclined to believe that when the Templars were arrested on September 13th 1307, some passer-by saw his chance and smashed it open, damaging the red stone which would have held the lock, then hauled it away in a cart to put on the front of his own manor somewhere. Whatever lay people were connected with the church would then have bricked it up as it is now and over the centuries forgot that it ever meant anything to anyone.

***

But you can try an experiment yourself with this 'False Door'. Get into whatever meditative mode you use, create whatever atmospheres you need via symbols or candles or lighting, build up its image and look into and through the door as you might with a scrying mirror or crystal ball.

I've done this numerous times with varying results – none of them spectacular or even worth noting. It's no use sharing these because the results – while interesting to me – are so trivial and I'm probably engineering them to appease my own inner-world view. Don't send your own results to me because I'll just steal them.

You see I'm acutely aware of the many seers I've read about over very many years whose researches into the past via the akashic records just don't add up. If you want a laugh and end up shaking your head in dismay at the antics of supposed Teachers, then read:

- David Conway's demolition of Grace Cooke's visions in his brilliant and waspish autobiography *Magic without Mirrors*.
- Gregory Tillet's shocking disclosures about Charles Webster Leadbeater in his *The Elder*

213

Brother. (Incidentally, I see Leadbeater as the occult world's equivalent of Jimmy Savile. He groomed Annie Besant who then indulged him in his passion for Messiahs – especially if they were little boys.

- Russell Miller's *Bare-Faced Messiah* for his exposé of L. Ron Hubbard which all would-be Scientologists should be forced to read without being declared Fair Game.

I digress.

If you apply this technique or similar toward the Templar Door then you might want to visualise yourself at midnight, ghosting through it and finding yourself in an empty room.

Actually, I'll rephrase that: '...and finding yourself in an Empty Room.' Trying to avoid too much of the kabbalibosh here, the concept of the Empty Room links with very deep Mysteries: in the darkness and nothingness, you can find *The All.* Well, I say 'very deep' but I'm probably being a bit pompous again, and suggesting I know a bit more than ordinary folks. I can feel Bill Gray trying to muscle in again but I won't let him.

In brief, there is a 'place' on the Tree of Life known as Daath, which means Knowledge. Its traditional correspondences are:

Image: Head with two faces, looking both ways
Planet/Star: Sirius
Virtues: Detachment. Perfection of Justice and the application of the Virtues untainted by personality or ego. Confidence in the Future
Vices: Doubt of the Future. Apathy, Inertia. Cowardice. Pride leading to isolation.

Titles: The Invisible Sephira; The Hidden; The Unrevealed
Spiritual Experience: Vision across the Abyss
Symbols: Prism; Cell; Empty Room; Sacred Mountaintop, Grain of Corn.

I'm sure that one of my readers might like to tackle that lot but you're on your own. I'm just sick of riding that destrier throughout this journey. So I'm visualising myself now with my back to the door at Alton Priors and sending our magickal steed off into the hillside, where I see it flowing into the lines of the white horse of Alton Barnes, which is what it has been all along.

But before I leave the Empty Room I'd recommend you to pick up that symbol of the grain of corn because it's about to become relevant.

***

I wrote earlier about my absurd but possibly genuine contact on the physical plane with an extra-terrestrial chappy outside of Poundland in the shopping centre. I'm beginning to think that this whole project is less to do with the Templars than a highly precise Spirit of Place – the actual field which extends beyond the Templar Door.

This is known simply as the East Field. I had no idea until I came to do this research that it has an undercurrent involving crop circles, mysterious lights, wild spirits and even an experiment involving a Close Encounter of the 5th Kind, organised by Dr. Stephen Greer.

***

A few decades ago I had an idea for a book which I thought might be a best-seller. I planned to list ALL the Templar sites within Britain and link them with the nearest druidic and pre-druidic and pre-pre-druidic Places of Power if I might use that term. I still assumed that the Order of the Poor Knights were, in their core, mighty adepts in touch with all sorts of secret, sacred sciences and telluric (I love that word!) energies. They would suss out places like Alton Priors and build their churches on them. At one time I was obsessed by tiny hamlet of Temple, in Somerset, where the knights would have overseen and owned the adjacent pagan summit of Cley Hill. The latter, traditionally the home of the King of Faery, and rumoured to contain caves and a golden ram, was later seen as a homing beacon for UFOs.

Why else, apart from the sheep, would Templars want land there? Quite simply the countryside is so filled with ancient things even today that wherever anyone built, they would have been neighbours to something.

Still, I do like to think that Ancuellos would have 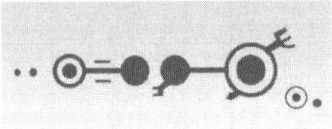 arrived at what is now the East Field with its babbling pond and stone circle and sensed energies beyond the ordinary.

And there is of course the matter of the Ark of the Covenant which I quickly want to dispose of. I'm not impressed by that either. Some writers have opined that it was this that the Huges de Payens and his mates found in their digs below the Temple of Solomon. I know of at least a dozen books revealing where it is now but you must track them down yourselves. Laurence Gardner said that it has been translated into another dimension, via the great maze within the Templar-inspired Chartres Cathedral.

Graham Phillips (one of my favourite authors) was drawn into an adventure that suggested it might have found its way to the lovely county of Shropshire. Others have described it as powerful mystic mechanism which could generate plasma and discharge it with devastating effect, rather like the almost-forgotten orgone accumulators of Wilhelm Reich.

As for this plasma (which apparently is *not* the same stuff that I sold for $10 a pint in Kentucky), Trevor James Constable argued in his book *The Cosmic Pulse of Life* that UFOs were not nuts and bolts spacecraft but amoeba-like lifeforms that inhabit the upper atmosphere. He thought of them as intelligent 'bioforms' held in a plasma state, existing usually within the invisible ranges of the electro-magnetic spectrum. That is, our atmosphere is full of invisible life forms and some places, like our East Field, seem to be more congenial to them than others.

Actually, I vaguely remember trying an experiment of something I saw on You Tube. It showed how you can make a plasma ball using half a grape, a glass and a microwave. Can't remember the details now. I think it worked. Certainly, it was a whole lot easier than trying to make an homunculus or a Moonchild.

Which brings me to the notion and the reality of Crop Circles.

***

I have **known** people who have crept into the fields at dark of night and created a crop circle using the most primitive equipment. They did so because they wanted to show that all the crop circle phenomena were hoaxes and delighted in any opportunity to humiliate the Cerealogists, as I think they're called these days.

I have also known *of* people who have crept into the fields at dark of night and created a crop circle using the most primitive equipment. They did so because they felt compelled, that they were reacting to impulses that were benign and linked to the Land itself. When you think about it, the farmer who fashioned the Alton Barnes White Horse in 1812 must have been acting on just such an impulse. Perhaps all of the White Horses in Wiltshire were the result of this sort of inner pressure.

Although I have seen many crop circles from afar I have never been inside one. I'm intrigued that among  those who have, their reactions were as varied as those who visited the Saxon Church in Bradford on Avon. That is, some felt spiritual delight; others, a marked unease, often with an unpleasant and lingering metallic taste. Of the two groups it's the latter which interests me the most. I know exactly what that 'unpleasant and lingering metallic taste' is like, having experienced it myself when I've tried to poke my vison into places where I shouldn't. Long Story *that* one!

If I have to get off the fence about all this, then…

I believe that many, if not most crop circles are created by energies (either from above or below) that we don't yet grasp. And when I say 'above' I don't necessarily mean interdimensional or trans-galactic spaceships. Even the staid Ministry of Defence once ventured that certain UFOs were actually 'buoyant plasmas' which they defined as exotic plasma constructs held together by electro-magnetic fields. And while we're at it, dipping briefly into areas of light relief, I believe that 60% of UFOs seen today are probably 'black projects' developed by governments making use of propulsion systems that the world should have had, and been enriched by, 50 years ago.

Just saying.

***

As I write this the season for crop circles isn't yet upon us, and the grain of corn you glimpsed in the Empty Room is still in the ground germinating away. But if you were to google images for 'Crop Circles Wiltshire' you'd see a variety of extraordinary glyphs, especially at Hackpen Hill that we visited earlier, in East Field itself, and another right next to the  Templar Door which got little publicity but made me go *Hmmm….*

All this sort of ties in with Steven Greer's 'Disclosure Project'. Dr. Steven Macon Greer is an American retired traumatologist and ufologist who founded the *Center for the Study of Extraterrestrial Intelligence* and the *Disclosure Project*, which seeks the disclosure of allegedly suppressed UFO information. Like everyone who enters this sort of field he has his detractors so you must make your own judgements.

The relevant yarn here is that he and circle of others stood in the East Field before the Templar Door, and attempted to make telepathic contact with whoever or whatever was 'up there', although I'm disappointed that none of them thought to borrow my bull-roarer. They became human equivalents of the Rollrights stone circle, using techniques that were purely from the realms mental magick. Each of them experienced a great circular non-physical craft descend and encircle them, so that the human individuals felt themselves to be inside the craft, humans interspersed with ETs, whose interest in humanity was benign, and whose expression was Love.

***

So here am I back at the Templar Door again and I must say that I feel weary. I've only got one more phase for this little 'journey' and that's next week when we go to visit the church at Garway, staying overnight in what promises to be an excellent Bed and Breakfast place on the very border with England and Wales – all the liminality I could hope for.

Although Amberaldus does seem to have some potential in my mind, I must say that Ancuellos hasn't really taken off within my psyche, although I suppose that's a good thing. Not sure that Margaret would approve of our table levitating as Philip did for the group which created him. Then again, it would need several people working at him as the Toronto group did, and surely to goodness people these days would have better things to do with their lives than that?

Once we get back from Garway I'll go round every room in our house and banish every last shred of

Templarness, and put my little stone in a nice place next to our pond among all the other 'sacred' stones we've accumulated there over the years.

Let it live among the faeries.

Believe you me, the Templars won't mess with *them…*

Chapter 17

In my beginning is our end…

Nearly done. I stumbled on a cracking Bed and Breakfast when searching on-line, near Garway. It promises cream teas on arrival, large rooms with views and seems to be set in a slightly lost but beautiful valley on the border between Wales and England. I won't give the name in case the landlady ever reads this and has a hissy fit and won't let us stay there again. I've assured Margaret that said woman will probably be a secret Templar who has waited a lifetime for our appearance. After I've spent all this time summoning, stirring and trying to evoke them all to some sort of visible appearance, this really is their last chance to get into my story.

That visit won't be until next week. I'm scribbling this while sitting in a recliner in a small shed at the bottom of our small garden. The very word 'shed' gives me a surge of pure delight because I fulfil all the clichés and stereotypes evoked (among the English at least) by the concept of Man and his Shed.

If you want, I can add an esoteric gloss to this: my shed is actually a manifestation of Daath's Empty Room, a very temple of gnosis within which I look both forward and back, the grain of Knowledge being planted within my psyche even as I sit and scribble and sip tea from a flask.

I think that's pretty clever.

Outside I can hear Meatloaf belting out his orisons. This is the name which we have given to the blackbird that allows us to share what is obviously *his* place. Last year he appeared as a scrawny fledgling and skittered around our feet with total disregard. This year he is a fat bastard who looks down on us with barely concealed contempt. But – ye gods – what a voice!

Further down the garden I can see Margaret, red-faced and sweating, standing on a chair and trimming the branches of a small tree which is apparently called a forsythia. I offer to get her a set of step-ladders but she just grunts. In fact she was equally tetchy earlier on when I was watching her mowing the lawn. I don't know why.

I blame the Templars.

***

When we go to Garway I will be looking for the sort of encounter described by Graham Phillips in his search for the Ark of the Covenant. While trying to fathom the codes hidden within the stained glass windows of All Saints Church at Burton Dassett, he was helped by the sudden and silent appearance of the churchwarden. This was not a spirit but a flesh and blood individual who gave him some crucial insights. The man was short, sixty-ish, with grey hair and beard. Phillips didn't hear him approach. After he had imparted some unexpected information he disappeared suddenly and silently when the author's back was turned.

As you might guess, although Phillips met him twice and was given important information each time, he never saw him again. As he commented:

> In fact, the vicar told me that no one matching his description was a churchwarden at All Saints Church. To be honest, the old man had never told me who he was. I had just assumed that he was a

churchwarden as he had been lighting candles and tending the flowers. Search as I might, I never saw the old man again and never discovered his identity. Whoever the man was, he clearly did not visit the church regularly, yet both times I had been there he was there to help. In fact, without him my research might never have gone as far as it did... What I can say is that there was something strange about the man I had taken to be a churchwarden. The first time I had met him he had somehow entered the church and snuck up behind me without my hearing a thing. Not only did the sound of footsteps on the stone floor of the building echo like crazy, but the church door creaked like hell.[1]

There has always been a tradition in the esoteric world of (apparently physical) Mysterious Strangers turning up to impart knowledge or change lives. I have read of people being convinced that they have met characters as diverse as Merlin, le Comte de St Germaine and various legendary alchemists who should have been dead for centuries. It is easy to mock this, but a quiet acceptance that such things might be possible in this Quantum Universe can give us back a sense of wonder that is all too often missing in our world. In short, I want to meet someone like that churchwarden when we go to Garway.

Have I already got a yarn of my own?

Yes...

***

In my last job before retirement I managed a specialist Mobile Library that visited the elderly in remote communities across Wiltshire. Once, on the edge of

Salisbury, I was parked up and sorting out my stock when a middle-aged priest appeared at the rear door. He was medium height, clean shaven with short grey hair and wore a black suit and dog-collar. I don't know enough about clerical garb to tell whether he was Protestant or Catholic, though I would guess the latter.

'Have you got a copy of the Gospel of Thomas?' he asked without preamble.

'No,' said I instantly, having an anal and comprehensive knowledge of my stock and anything remotely wacky therein. 'But I can order one for you.'

He looked at me. I looked at him. Some people have the ability to radiate *presence* – whatever that might be or how it might be caused. This man oozed it.

'I believe it to be true.'

I'd never read it, had no opinion and could only offer again to order a copy.

'No need. I believe it to be true,' he repeated, with slightly added emphasis.

I turned away to have a quick look at my religious books to see if I could tempt him with something else (and also boost up the numbers and issues on which the service depended), but when I turned back he was gone. No sight of him anywhere.

A pity. I rather liked him too.

***

Now I'm NOT totally off-piste here so bear with me. The Gospel of Thomas was discovered near Nag Hammadi, Egypt, in December 1945. Supporters argue that it is at least as old and as valid as the accepted Gospels. It opens with Logion 1 which says:

I who write this am Thomas,
the Double, the Twin.
Yeshua, the Living Master spoke,
and his secret sayings I have written down.

I assure you, whoever grasps their
Meaning will not know the taste of death.

The Gospel as a whole seems to declare that the Kingdom of God exists upon the earth today if people just open their eyes. There is 'divine light' within all of us, which allows us to see the Kingdom of God in our physical surroundings. I can go along with that much.

The relevance to this project is that there are dozens of speculations as to what the Treasure of the Templars – and also the Treasure of the Cathars – really was. A few lone voices have suggested that it might have been an explosive, forgotten and Secret Gospel, possibly even this Gospel of Thomas.

I have a copy now and I'll put it to the test. I close my eyes, open the book at random and jab my finger onto a Logion to see what it says. It descends on Logion 43 which says:

His students said to him,
Who are you to
be saying
such things to us?"
Yeshua replied,

'Do you not realize who I am
from everything I have said to you?
Have you come to be like the Judeans
who either accept the tree,

227

but reject its fruit, or welcome the fruit
and despise the tree?'

That means nothing to me. I did it twice more, turning the book around and upside down. Each time the same Logion.

Yes yes yes I know that this is probably a pointless exercise for myself and most people, but I'll guarantee that one day someone will write to me and say: *Actually*...

While I'm intrigued by the Gospel of Thomas because of its alternative and even heretical reputation I can't see why anyone – Templars or Cathars – would risk their lives for it. Even if it *was* the Secret Gospel giving the true teachings of Jesus you'll not get me accepting that he was any more than a man – although I'll allow that he might have been a red-hot magickal Adept. But no more so than Simon Magus and Helen, and *their* teacher John the Baptist, who might also have been Jesus and the Magdalen's teacher.

***

Before we go to Garway next week I've already done all the research both on-line and in the library, though I haven't told M that. When Aldous Huxley was invited to any gathering during his years in America he would spend the evening before boning up on a particular topic in his encyclopaedia. At the party, he would then lead the conversation by subtle stages until someone was effectively tricked into mentioning that topic. Huxley would then launch into a brilliant and apparently spontaneous lecture. Among the socialites, he had the reputation for being omniscient.

You can see my plan for Garway, can't you? When I get there I will impress Margaret with my innate, intuitive knowledge of its architecture and history.

*How do you **know** all that?* She will exclaim with amazement. I will shrug modestly. *I just do...* I will say, letting my voice trail off shyly while looking at the ground then walking on.

Mind you, I begin to think that she sees through me. So until then, here is what I've already learned...

***

The actual site for the preceptory was probably due to the springs rising from nearby Garway Hill providing both drinking water and supplies for the fishponds. St. Michael's church, Garway, is one of only six churches in England built by the Knights Templar and is the most substantial, apart from Temple Church in London. The latter was bombed during the war and rebuilt; Temple Church in Bristol was bombed and left as a shell. St Michael's is the real thing. After all these telesmic figures and inner pathworkings and redundant church shells, I really do want to see the real thing at the last.

The original nave would have been round but there are few traces of this because, after the suppression in 1307, in common with most of their property, Garway passed to  the sister Order of the Knights of St John (the Hospitallers, in whom I've shown a spectacular lack of interest) in 1326. They replaced the nave with a more conventional rectangular one during the 15th Century. This was probably due to subsidence.

The imposing tower seems to have been built in  1180 to replace what was believed to be a wooden Celtic church dating back to as early as 600 AD. This tower was originally separate from the rest of the church and designed for defensive purposes, as can be seen from its massive size, the paucity of window openings especially in the lower stage and the palpable strength of the masonry. Sadly, this tower is no longer open to anyone but all the sources insist that the interior is simple and conceals no exciting architectural features that might suggest Sacred Geometries, although the nearby dovecote is said to have 666 holes.

Henry II granted this site to the Templars, possibly because he wanted to have an elite military Order established so close to the lawless Welsh borders. The local area - known as Archenfield - was a relatively peaceful buffer state between the two countries, located in England but with the people Welsh-speaking.

The nave is 13th Century and contains pews, dating back to the 17th century It is quite rare to find original pews in Churches today, as prior to that date the parishioners were made to stand in Church, on the basis of 'no pain, no gain'. The font is 14th Century and – according to the leaflet - features Hospitaller iconography of a serpent - associated with healing - twined around a cross.

The chancel arch is Norman and dates to the Templar foundation. This is of three orders. The outer order is the traditional Norman chevron, the inner made with surprisingly Moorish-style voussoirs (wedge-shaped stones). This Oriental-style design was a result of the Templar contact with Eastern design and architectural style in the Holy Land.

On the left of this arch is what is described as a wonderful carving of a Green Man, although I'm tempted

to believe that the term 'Green Man' is used because the worshippers knew nothing about Baphomet.

The roof was constructed by the Hospitallers in around 1400. There is a 13th Century arcade that leads to the South Chapel which dates from the Templars but which was substantially reconstructed in 16th Century after the Hospitallers had relinquished the site during the dissolution of the monasteries. The external walls are rich with carved figures and are notable for an intriguing collection of mason's marks, including a Maltese cross, a swastika, the Lamb of God, a Patriarchal Cross, Cross Fourchee, a winged dragon, and a rather *touching Dextra Dei*, or Hand of God, emerging from a cloud. There are carvings of a sword, believed of course to be Templar, a fish and a snake. And also numerous examples of carved

Templar coffin lids, which were reused as steps and window lintels by the Hospitallers, which is pretty damned insulting if you ask me. I've never liked them.

Garway also controlled extensive but scattered properties elsewhere in south-western Herefordshire. Apparently remote and cut off from major communication routes, Garway was a far less wealthy commandery than those in eastern England. Yet the man himself, Jacques de Molay, the Grand Master made his way there in 1294 to do – goodness knows what. Probably nothing at all in any esoteric sense. Possibly just saying Hello, or - if he had any mystical intimation of his fate - to say Goodbye.

He certainly didn't come for the sort of cash that the French King Philip IV was so desperate for. In the first nine months after the Templars' arrest in England (10 January to 29 September 1308), the income received at Garway was only £871. 40s. 2½d. This was less than half of the income of £1811. 9s. 1¾d received at the important commandery of Temple Bruer in Lincolnshire, in eastern England, during the same period.

At the time of the Templars' arrests in 1308 there were only two Templars living at Garway, Philip de Meux, knight, and William de Pokelington. Only one Templar who was interrogated in the British Isles, William of Hereford, claimed to have been received here, ten years before 27 January 1310. The only other mention of Garway during the trial proceedings emphasized its remoteness: in his final 'confession' the priest-brother John of Stoke placed his alleged second reception ceremony at Garway, on 30 November 1293.

Philip de Meux, the last Templar preceptor in Herefordshire, was tortured and charged with heresy. Both he and William de Pokelington admitted to false beliefs and publicly confessed. They were absolved and accepted back into the Church.

Garway does not seem to have been an actual hot-bed of Templardom during the final decade or so. Perhaps the bulk of them escaped in time, leaving only those two to face the thumbscrews.

***

In his rather compelling website *View from the Big Hills*, the blogger 'Celtic Fire' (who really knows his stuff) describes the Welsh Marches as a strange and magical hinterland.

> Like many borderland areas, it is rich in its history and mythology. *The Battle of Evermore*, written and performed by Led Zeppelin and accompanied by Sandy Denny, truly captures the in-between nature of this part of Britain in a way that few other artists have been able to. Cheltenham singer song-writer Johnny Coppin also managed to nail it with some of his music.[2]

I'm rather hoping for a bit of this borderland liminality when we're up there. As I described it in my collection of essays *Short Circuits*, I experienced an hour of what I can only call 'dual consciousness' when boating up the River Wye, not far from Garway. As best as I can explain I inhabited the mind of, well…myself. But in a parallel life. That life was similar to but somewhat divergent from my own. Perhaps it was the life I could have taken had I made certain choices much earlier on. I can only assume that Parallel Alan was as equally bewildered to find himself in the head of someone travelling up the a river in a boat, as I was to find myself sitting in his kitchen looking out at the BMW on his driveway.

The tour guide on the boat had explained that the rocks on one side were England, those on the other were of Wales. On our trip up to Garway, staying exactly on the borderland between both countries, I'm keen to experience this sort of thing again.

***

Before we set off I got out my very old Waite-Rider tarot pack and asked: 'When we come back from Garway and this whole journey is finished, what card might express my overall feeling?'

The card which appeared was **Judgemen**t, which pretty much sums up the whole project: the dead souls rising from their graves, the cold distant mountains that I saw in my dream that 'soldiers from another dimension' would help me cross, and the angel bearing the Cross of St George that was so important to the English Templars. For the kabbalists, using the system of correspondences devised by W.G. Gray, then this card aligns with the path between Chokmah and Binah and is really, if you look at all the associations, a perfect summary of my Templar journey. It also tells me quite clearly what I have to do when I get back.

On also asking, effectively, 'What else?' the pack told me that we would meet a friendly dark young man, exemplifying the Knight of Wands. When Margaret asked what Garway would mean for her, she got the Four of Wands, which according to Waite predicts: '…country life, repose, concord, harmony, prosperity and peace.' I take this to mean that once the Templars are out of my head then our home and lives will get back to the sort of calm that is priceless.

I'll let you know.

The little Duo-Lingo owl has just popped up. it warns me that because I haven't accessed the programme for some time my fluency level will be reduced, and I'm advised to start again.

Bof, Zut, Putain, Con, Branleur, Fils de Pute and Mal de Mer! I won't take this lying down. *Suis-je un homme ou une omelette !!??*

I blame the Templars.

***

The night before we set off I sent out the signal again:

> If there are any Templars or Templar energies
> (past or present) in the Garway area then make
> yourselves known to us in any symbolic way.

In other words, all omens gratefully accepted as tokens of currency between the worlds. Though, as with synchronicities, I won't get too worked up and run through the Welsh Marches crying *Hosannas* if and when they appear.

***

Today is Saturday the 16th of June and I'm sitting in the window seat of our B & B looking out the solitary Red Kite launching from its nest in a nearby tree and circling around the Monnow Valley. Margaret is lying on the bed and quietly doing some of Olive Pixley's 'Armour of Light' exercises before we set off for St Michael's Church at Garway. If you don't know what these exercises are then you might want to find out. They are very odd, but also very powerful.

The B & B (I will name it after all) is called 'Part Y Seal'. Having met the owners and experienced the 'tone' of of their place – entirely Oriental – I don't for one moment think they'd object to a couple of Templar Groupies. Even they don't know what Part y Seal actually means, and scholars of Welsh in Cardiff have been flummoxed too. I noticed a crest on the side of the house with the Latin motto under it which read *Cavendo Tutus*, which means Safety through Caution, but I'm not sure how that applies to me at the moment. Still, the place itself had all the peace and beauty we could have wished for. Especially for Margaret, after the draining torments of her times in Gomorrah. And for me it had a curiously wistful and almost sad *fin de siècle* atmosphere, as if it wasn't going to last much longer, so absorb it while you can.

Yesterday, before we set out, I suggested to M that she too should approach the next couple of days in the same way as me: see everything that happens as a secret dealing between herself and her innermost deities.

She didn't say 'Bollocks' this time.

After sending out that before-sleep signal – or was it challenge? – we did indeed have numerous little benign incidents yesterday that seemed to indicate a 'meant to be' that enveloped our journey. In particular we made an unplanned visit to nearby Kilpeck and arrived at the exact moment a lady started giving a lecture within the church as to its significance. She was wielding a large 'stang' of the sort used by the Clan of Tubal Cain, whose Magister Robert Cochrane was one of the many folk that Bill Gray fell out with. In brief, witches use the Stang in various ways including representing the Horned One, aiding in spirit flight, and directing energies. We stood at the back and listened and learned a lot as she  began by saying that this place was sacred long before Christianity. She also pointed out the carving on the amazing doorway of the almost hidden Rainbow Man that was important to Margaret in her own Work and the numerous Templar symbols within and without.

As with Orchardleigh, I think it would be easy for me to get sucked into this place. I didn't stay to hear the end of the lady's talk because my mobile phone rang inside the church. Nobody *ever* rings me. I only keep the device for the emergencies. I ran outside among the graves and saw on the phone's screen the large letters **Virgin**. It was my internet provider ringing from a call centre in, from his accent, some Himalayan mountain fastness, wanting to know if… I pressed the red button and hung up before he could finish.

You're having a joke, lads, I said to the spirits of the Templars.

Outside, however, Margaret yet again saw the outline of sealed-up doorway in the north wall.

That was yesterday. No sign of the Knight of Wands but I'm beginning to wonder if that might be me. I'm happily sitting here in the window-seat after an almost sleepless but strangely happy night of what I can only call 'whiteness'. That doesn't make sense, even to me, but it's the best I can explain. I don't feel tired at all.

Before I'd gone to bed and tried to sleep I'd sent out a signal to Amberaldus or anyone else, allowing him to come through – though preferably not by visible appearance. Nothing of that sort happened. I had two dreams, neither of the startling. In one I was making a series of small, flimsy Tardises out of thin card. (To non-Brits the Tardis is the time machine used by the television character of Dr Who.) I suppose the dream was spot-on in that respect: this whole book has been a series of small, thin, time travelling episodes. The second dream, which wasn't as disturbing as it sounds, was of me finding the body of headless female in shallow water. Goodness knows what that might mean.

I'd been re-reading Melusine Draco's book *Starchild* last night. Melusine, aka Suzanne Ruthven, is one of the Real Ones who has always seen through me. Many years ago, when I was single, she seduced me on the astral plane in an act which was unexpected, much needed and extremely satisfying – the little minx! In her book, however, she points out that the iron in our blood, the calcium in our bones, the oxygen in our very breath were all forged in the deep and blistering heart of stars before they exploded. So we are – all of us – directly connected, we are all stardust made flesh.

Perhaps that is the connection I will try to make with the spirits of the Templars in Garway itself, that perhaps we all contain essences from the same, silvery star which exploded a billion years ago.

It is still June 16th and we are home now, unpacked – didn't take long. I'm sure all sorts of cosmically important events happened on this date but I don't need to chase that up now.

When we set off for Garway from Part y Seal a strong wind blew up and rattled the trees and set all the crows off under the leaden skies and I rather hoped for an apocalyptic storm but it quickly calmed. I think M might have muttered something to Them. We crossed the River Monnow which, because we were on the exact borderland is also called Afon Mynwy. I didn't get any sense of dual consciousness this time or any profound liminality but the scenery along the one-lane road was to die for and a huge hawk flew across our path.

The church itself was down a very narrow with no parking. I did a 43-point turn in our car between the hedgerows to face the right way when we exited.

When we arrived, there was a lovely female churchwarden attending to the flowers but she was very much a flesh and blood being, and not like the mysterious chappy Graham Phillips encountered.

'I'll leave you alone' she said, and she did, and we had the place to ourselves, and I must say it was all I had hoped to find, and Margaret agreed. Garway really was the real thing.

I said the things I needed to say to the Order as a whole, then to Philip de Meux, William de Pokelington and Jacques de Molay himself, who had stood in this same place and touched the same carvings and nodded his approval. I had a sense of how pleased the building itself, the very land beneath would have been to have the great Jacques de Molay come all that way, to the very edge of things, to see it all.

Then Margaret took the lead with the next bit...

We drew red hearts on the palms of our hands to match the Templar graffiti, both knowing that it might not have meant the same to them as it does to the whole world today. She then created and wove around us a private little magick in that holy space, hand to hand, eye to eye, heart-centres awakened and passing light between us, expanding and then sending it out. I did what she said, as she has the power. That's all you need to know; the details wouldn't make it work for anyone else. Like a lover's kiss, a lover's smile, it is the spontaneity and feeling that does the trick and makes the world glow. In there, in that empty room, we made our own magick and had even been provided with fresh flowers to do so.

Separately, we silently blessed the Templars and all those who had been punished because of them. I whispered the Paternoster (just in case) and I must say it felt very good to utter *Non nobis Domine, non nobis, sed nomini tuo da gloriam* into the empty room with its high rafters and multitude of six-pointed stars decorating its heights. Then we said the Pax Vobiscum and left by the side door, which the churchwarden lady insisted we must use.

Outside, Margaret saw – yet again - a sealed door-frame in the northern wall to match that of Alton Priors and the partial remains of one at Kilpeck. Again, I'd never have noticed. We saw the *Winged Griffin* but couldn't find the *Dexter Dei.* Perhaps after all my shenanigans the Hand of God didn't want to reveal itself to me. I won't worry about that. Goodness know what the Griffin symbolised but I want it to know that I'm on its side.

***

It's all over now. What have I gained from this? I'm not sure.

I've clarified my thoughts (or do I mean torments?) about the Light and the Dark and confirmed my suspicions that the Templars were very ordinary human beings first and Creatures of Myth much further down the time-lines in ways that might have surprised them. I think that in studying their Order I've balanced my own ideas regarding deities and destinies, bloodlines and beliefs. After that first visit to Alton Priors with Margaret I feel that I've passed through an invisible door into the stillness of my own Empty Room, where all formal worship is redundant and whatever I need in terms of Truth is below my feet, not up in my head.

There have been a lot of synchronicities and unusual individuals turning up while writing all this (far more than I've chronicled here) but I've had these all my life and I find that they rarely lead anywhere and may well mean nothing at all.

I can visualise Ancuellos clear as day but he has not yet, as WGG suggested, been energised by inner beings. For that to happen I would have had to work at the telesmic body with a passion for the project that I don't really have. I hope that my readers don't feel short-changed by that or taken for a ride. Perhaps Ancuellos was never meant to be more than an exemplar – or even just a suggestion of possibility. Perhaps Ancuellos is a *ren* for the use of others, not me.

On the other hand, 'Amberaldus' creates the sort of frisson that suggests an inner being knocking on that invisible door. If so, he can bugger off...

If I could sum up in one word the atmosphere engendered by writing this whole book, it would have to be 'Unpleasant'. I asked Margaret if she wanted to say anything about the writing of this book about this and she wrote:

> Alan tells me that this book was written with a light touch. He also tells me it was fun in places. I have to confess I didn't see that fun. There seems to have been a heavy, irritable, anxious and scattered energy hanging around our house. It sometimes felt like it was twisting Alan physically in some way, locking up his neck and shoulders and giving him what we referred to as 'Templar head'. I want to feel compassion for the scared, lost, cheated souls he was dealing with, and to some extent I do. I am glad that they can move on though now, and hopefully in more peace. I'm looking forward to reclaiming the

house and garden as the much loved and tranquil oasis it was!

Hmmm…

The Templars were ordinary fellas who backed the wrong horse and lost everything, yet goodness knows we've all made *that* mistake. To that extent I feel a fondness that I will make sure is neither based on pity nor on being patronising. Even so, by their very demise they created legends. In the eyes of some became almost more than human: magickal Adepts with secret gnosis that could have destroyed their known world.

The fact that they were initiated into an Order means nothing. The fact that some of them were High Initiates and ultimately Grand Masters means nothing. In the late 19th early 20th Century the likes of Blavatsky, Besant, Bailey and the dreadful Charles Webster Leadbeater (not to mention all of Freemasonry) were obsessed with the idea of Initiates and almost drooled at the thoughts of Templars. It was as if the very act of ceremonial/ritual initiation conferred or confirmed a degree of spiritual exaltation greater than ordinary humans could possess. Even today, in 2018, I still find people who are taken in by this.

The truth is, in my long life, I've met people who live modestly and quietly, whose jobs are often described as 'menial', yet who have more psychic gifts and show greater wisdom and understanding than the various Adeptii I know who blow their own trumpets. None of them spoke to their peers about their own extraordinary inner lives, yet they were/are further ahead on the path than the Outer Plane Ineptii can possibly imagine.

Oh gosh… I think I'm on a high horse.

Rant over.
Sorry 'bout that.

***

Today is Father's Day, June 17th. This morning, in brief, I spent some time building up the image of All Saints Church in Alton Priors in its Templar heyday. I saw the splendid oak door in the north wall and, within my Body of Light, opened it without knocking. Inside, by the light of very large candles and a few oil lamps, the half-dozen or so knights seemed to be having a meeting. They seemed surprised – or perhaps puzzled - to see me. I made my way to the front, to the altar, then turned to face them.

I bade them peace, asked for their blessings, and warned them to make themselves *very* scarce before Friday 13th of October 1307.

Then I left by the same door.

Did that *really* happen? Well it happened within me, within my own multiverse, so that's reality enough for my life.

If it worked, maybe they saw me as a spirit from the future, as Dolores Cannon experienced with her co-workers when they made contact with Nostradamus. I just hope that somehow, in some realm of possibility, I managed to help at least one of 'my' Templars on the edge of this Wiltshire field.

Then, to finish off, I went around our whole house and tried to get rid any of these niggling Templar energies that seem to have been invoked and which Margaret was more attuned to than myself. I took Raven and used the

Banishing Ritual that William G. Gray perfected, relating to Time/Space/Events. (If you're unfamiliar with this - and most are - then I've given a shortened version in the final Appendix.) And ***then*** I gave it all another layer of peace by using our magick bell.

Once the house felt pure I took the templarish stone and put it among the others next to our little pond

***

I am sitting on a recliner in my shed now, with both doors open and a flask of tea at hand. It is sunny, perfect. I have sucked into myself all the rest of the little symbols and icons and mandalas and burned them into motes of nothingness in the column of fire within my spine, and the air before me is pure and the world is white again.

Soon, our four daughters will arrive and make a procession down our long and narrow garden to lay a variety of unusual and unlikely Father's Day gifts at my feet, as though I were an old hoary god from a near-forgotten worship from the Land of the Ever-Young. They will take the mickey ruthlessly and I will glow, and hold out my open palm to them which still has the image of the heart upon it.

Pax Vobiscum I say to the universe and the Templars for a final time, then settle back in my chair and listen to the song of the blackbird and try to find my own peace.

Footnotes

Chapter 1   *The Invisible Door*
[1] I prefer this spelling because it looks arcane. I am NOT a Thelemite

Chapter 2   *Listening to Echoes*
[1] Quoted from *The Aryan Christ,* by Richard Noll.
[2] *The Knights Templar – the History and Myths of the Legendary Military Order*. Sean Martin

Chapter 3   *Templars and their Women*
[1] The ones in this area today are just ordinary fellas, who like dressing up and wearing badges. I wouldn't have them around to my place

Chapter 4   *Creating Ghosts*
[1] *The Templar Revelation*, Lynn Picknett and Clive Prince. Bantam Press.
[2] *Letters of Light*, Skylight Press

Chapter 5   *Dreams and Earthbounds*
[1] The laudable and formidable Fraternity of the Inner Light – of which I'm NOT a member.

Chapter 6   *And… Faery?!*
[1] http://eprints.uwe.ac.uk/25679/12/FBB4.pdf

Chapter 7   *'In the end is my beginning'*

Chapter 8   *Sins and their Echoes*
[1] I wrote *Inner Celtia* about this with the Welsh poet David Annwn.
[2] http://www.goddessandgreenman.co.uk/beltane

Chapter 9   *The White World*
[1] Some years ago I also wrote a dark comic novel about them called *Dark Light*, which I feel guilty about now.

Chapter 10   *Holy Hiatus*
[1] see *WyrdWood – the story of Dusty Miller* by Michael Kelly, Create Space.
[2] http://www.historyinanhour.com/2014/06/29/william-marshal-historys-greatest-knight/

Chapter 11   *At the Name of…*

[1] *The Templar Revelation*, Christopher Knight and Robert Lomas

[2] *Le Royaume du Graal* p 229

Chapter 12   *The Good People*

[1] *The Head of God*, Keith Laidler. Weidenfield page 187

[2] And yes, for the sake of my grandchildren I voted OUT.

Chapter 13   *At the Head Quarters*

[1] D.H. Lawrence

[2] Third occult hint. Anyone who denies them thrice will never get to Amenti.

Chapter 14   *White Horses and their ilk*

Chapter 15   *Sovereignty...*

[1] www.esotericbooks.com

[2] https://www.youtube.com/watch?v=s6YE4PCRNwc

[3] https://upliftconnect.com/marrying-the-land/

[4] https://www.mollylarkin.com/what-if-our-leaders-would-marry-the-land/

[5] Both titles by Skylight Press

[6] *To Think Without Fear,* Anthony Duncan. Skylight Press

Chapter 16   *Circles and their Crops*

Chapter 17   *In my beginning is our end...*

[1] *Templars and the Ark of the Covenant* p 212. Graham Phillips.

[2] https://viewfromthebighills.blogspot.com

Appendix 1

Esoteric Tomes and Ripping Yarns

The Secret Initiation of Jesus at Qumran: The Essene Mysteries of John the Baptist
by Robert Feather

During excavations near the Qumran ruins, one of the main translators of the Dead Sea Scrolls, Father Milik, had excavated a headless corpse that he believed to be that of John the Baptist. Robert Feather, who translated the Copper Scroll, tracked down the site of this grave and found physical evidence that led him to draw the same conclusion - that this is the final burial place of John the Baptist. Feather demonstrates a strong link between the Qumran Essenes and the writings in the New Testament and argues that both John the Baptist and Jesus were intimately involved in the community. He also suggests that the belief of early Christians in one true God was, in fact, based on a belief system centred around a form of monotheism, which was first formulated by the Egyptian Pharaoh, Akhenaten - and uniquely espoused by the Essenes at Qumran.

The Head Of God: The Lost Treasure of the Templars
by Keith Laidler

Keith Laidler set out to follow the travels of the sacred Templar Head known as Baphomet to its eventual resting place in Rosslyn, where he is certain it lies to this day. He argues, convincingly, that this had to be the head of Jesus. At the time when the Templars were suppressed for heresy, in a era when

Holy Relics were huge money-makers, several churches in Europe claimed to have the head of John the Baptist without any qualms or criticism or censure from Rome. However if they, beyond doubt, that the Templars really did have the head of Jesus then this would be proof, beyond doubt, that the Holy Catholic Church and it's belief in the divinity of Jesus and his resurrection was a sham.

The only two quibbles I have is that he makes a slight, passing reference to the Great White Brotherhood, which I don't believe in. He also refers to the head-cult in the courts of Akhenaten but I'm not sure there ever was one.

The Divine Deception: The Church, the Shroud and the Creation of a Holy Fraud
by Keith Laidler

More of the same, except that he makes a convincing argument that the figure on the Shroud of Turin was a medieval photograph (entirely possible and convincingly argued) made by the Templars, using the severed head of Jesus superimposed on the body of a crucified man. He also shows that the Shroud contains other pictures too, that few have commented upon, showing that it was certainly not one that ever wrapped the body of Jesus.

Don't knock these ideas until you read all his arguments.

The Second Messiah: Templars, the Turin Shroud & the Great Secret of Freemasonry
by Christopher Knight and Robert Lomas

Knight and Lomas, two high-grade Freemasons, argue

that the figure on the Shroud of Turin was actually that of Jacques de Molay, who was rumoured at the time to be the promised Messiah, and guardian of the secret teachings of Jesus which went back to pre-Akhenaten eras. As the blurb says: 'Using the latest scientific techniques, the authors prove that the shroud Molay was wrapped in is the one now known as the Turin Shroud.'

I think Laidler's arguments shade theirs, but not wholly. And as freemasons they show compelling links between the demise of the Templars and their survival within the Craft, not to mention the origin of the Craft and derring-do among the pharaohs.

The Templar Revelation: Secret Guardians of The True Identity Of Christ
Clive Prince and Lynn Picknett

I don't accept for one moment that the figure on the Shroud was that of Leonardo, made by himself using the early techniques in photography that were certainly possible. Much as I admire almost everything else about their other books, especially their demolition of the nonsense around the Priory of Sion, I'm not convinced by anything they say about de Vinci and his work. Putting all that aside however, they dig deeper than the previous authors into the background of the Templars, Cathars, and finally back to the ideas and beliefs of the first century AD and a devastating new view of the real character and motives of the founder of Christianity and the roles of John the Baptist and Mary Magdalene. And, once again, back to the source of these things in Ancient Egypt. A place which has a lot to answer for. Again, to use the blurb: 'They reveal nothing less than a secret history, preserved through the centuries but encoded in works of art and even in the great Gothic cathedrals, whose revelation could shake the foundations of the Church.'

The Templars and the Ark of the Covenant: The Discovery of the Treasure of Solomon

by Graham Phillips

Graham Phillips uncovered evidence that 13th-century Templars found the Ark and the Stones of Fire that were on the breast plate used by the High Priest, and that they brought these treasures back to central England when they fled the persecution. The author followed ciphered messages left by the Templars in church paintings, inscriptions, and stained-glass windows that led him to what may well be three of the Stones of Fire. When examined by Oxford University scientists these stones were found to possess odd physical properties that interfered with electronic equipment and produced a sphere of floating light similar to ball lightning. 'The Bible asserts that the Ark had the power to destroy armies and bring down the walls of cities. Now Graham Phillips provides scientific evidence that these claims may be true and offers compelling documentation that the Ark may be located in the English countryside, not far from the birthplace of William Shakespeare at Stratford-upon-Avon.'

He is one of my favourite authors in this field. If I envy any books particularly, they are his – with only one exception.

Finally, if you want a clear, sane book then you must get...

The Knights Templar: The History and Myths of the Legendary Military Order
By Sean Martin

As the blurb says, better than I could: 'With clarity and ease, Martin navigates between the orthodox and the speculative, the historical and the myth, to bring alive the story of the Templars.' And of course, he also had the balls to publish my black comic novel: *Dark Light – a Neo-Templar Time Storm.*

Appendix 2

The un-Holy Grail

The quest for the Holy Grail has occupied the spiritual life of Western people for centuries now. The attainment of the Grail - whatever it is - has been seen as the ultimate achievement within our experience. The Grail leads us into those purer realms from which there is no need of return. Attain the Grail and the material world is left behind forever.

Now there is perhaps more Grail-related literature on the bookshelves today than for any other spiritual impulse, and more academic light being directed toward the whole Arthurian cultus than any other topic within the Western Tradition. Countless theories expound upon the true nature of the Grail and the "Grail experience" - all of which must enable us to get a little closer to the thing itself. But there is still one Grail Secret which has scarcely been touched upon at all. It is a secret that is at once obvious, simple, and - like the Emperor's clothes - once revealed can never be ignored again.

Imagine, then, that we are witnessing the Grail Ceremony as it is retold in those basic versions which lurk aback of the popular consciousness... the small room in the enchanted castle, the two pure, sinless, chaste and perfect knights Galahad and Perceval, the mystic communion with the spear dripping blood into the Grail itself, and outside, peering through the window, the gaunt face of Lancelot - denied the experience through his regal sins.

Everyone knows this story. Everyone thrums to it at some time. But now consider this, and answer honestly:

Which modern person with any warmth, heart and passion could really give a damn about those two boring, virginal little prigs? Who could care about the chaste and sinless heaven that they would seek to enter? And, all those tedious esoteric sophistries apart, who could really care about the Grail itself if such dreariness is what it demands?

Galahad and Perceval are dead fish - the last surges of the Piscean Era drawing into itself - and the Grail is their vessel. Like any other spiritual experience the Grail Vision is something that the Western world should have let flow through, and then on, with appropriate blessings. Instead, we have clung to it. And to cling to any spiritual experience is to create a tyranny for ourselves. In its own luminous, beautiful, and impossibly pure way, the Holy Grail has held the inner life of the West in thrall for a long time now.

But that is not the last/lost secret of the Grail Ceremony. That is to be found, not in Galahad or Perceval or the Grail itself, but through the "face in the window." It is the great du Lac who holds those formulae which will take us into the next Age. An Age when the Grail will retreat to its proper place - although this smacks of occult heresy even to suggest such a thing. But if coming Ages cast their shadows before, then Lancelot is the foreshadowing of that Man Carrying Water who will stride us into Aquarius.

Though be aware that this is not going to happen soon. Forget all the shining eyed New Age, smashey and nicey attitudes. The sun will not arise in the constellation of Aquarius for another 300 years or so. Until then, we're stuck in that damned chalice with those cold fish, and we have to reach beyond the rim.

There is no suggestion here that Lancelot of the Lake ever had any historical basis, although attempts have been made to identify him as an alter ego of Gawaine, the "Hawk of May." Taught by enchantresses in a submarine world, Lancelot rose from the waters by his own impulse - imagery which is extremely important for those who understand. He is very much a creature of the Green Ray, a son of the Celtic Otherworld, and although this seems incongruous, it is a fact that military people are especially good at exploring the depths of this Ray. They have the discipline to get back, which many lack. They understand something of its cruelty, too.

Lancelot may well be a very potent faery being on the inner planes with his/its own uncompromising agenda. But for most of us he can best be seen as strata of consciousness, which can be reached, via the telesmic imagery of his Myth.

Contact with du Lac is unmistakable: a brooding sort of compassion; a grave kind of sympathy; the grizzled heart of a simple man made wise by a lifetime of battles, both within and without. There are hints of darkness, flashes of cruelty, and a capacity for ruthlessness as a last resort.

It is not a contact that can be sustained for long, nor is it an intellectual contact. Intelligent and simple, yes; intellectual and sophisticated, most definitely not. Yet it shows us a Way - narrow and fraught though It is - which can lead us into Wonder. It is the path of the warrior who chooses his Queen, the archetypal Woman, above any other revelation, and who will forsake the Christ-centred Heaven for another sort of reality.

In this wise, a study of that dragon legend of the Laidly Worm, which links with his castle in Northumberland, will repay the effort a thousand times. It was originally named Castle Dolorous; when he fell in love with Guinevere, he renamed it Joyous Gard. You can almost give your heart to him because of his sheer hopefulness. Lancelot may have been the creation of medieval story-tellers, but the magickal impulse behind him is ancient.

Because he can be contacted using a telesmic image, it is quite permissible to make plays upon his name. Thus Lancelot du Lac = Lance à l'eau du Lac, with the simple but tantalising connotations that this holds. And with Lancer meaning "to throw," then Lancer L'eau brings us back to the image of Aquarius pouring out the water from his pitcher. And again there is *Lance* and *lot* meaning luck or chance. The Lance of Destiny? The Spear of Luck? There is an arcanum concealed there too. This is certainly weak translation but the magick behind it is strong.

And we can wonder, too, at his very "Frenchness." Britain and France have a tanist relationship. In primordial times there was no sea between them and they shared, of course, the same rock strata. If we could, in some sense, reach that bedrock under the sea of our national consciousness, then we would reach a common level in which things Gallic would seep into our visions and dreams. This does in fact happen when a certain Magickal Current is touched, although it is a topic too complex to go into here. Likewise, when the two nations have recurring ideas about uniting politically, as Churchill suggested in 1940, or via physical means such as bridges or tunnels, then we can be sure that this same Current is being activated and worked right fiercely.

There is nothing cozy or cute about the du Lac contact, then. Nor is it easy to fix, for it seems to oscillate somewhere between those qualities needed to be the

Guardian for the Realms of the Queen at one extreme, and the dark heart of the Sacrificial Priest "who knows things" at the other. But make the contact and you will be touching the very pulse of the Aquarian Age, with all the love and terror and marvel it will hold.

Appendix 3

Extracted from *Magical Ritual Methods* by William G. Gray, Helios Books 1969

We can now improve our zeroing technique. Using a plain rod about 32 inches long, we face East (Magical East is always front, whichever way we stand) and hold the rod something like a rifle at the 'present arms'. Its lower end is kept close to the solar plexus with the left hand, the right hand gripping it so that the extended forefinger is about level with tip of nose. Quieten breathing and take a slow inhalation. Direct attention to point of rod. Now begin to turn deosil while pushing rod down to horizontal position with right hand (near end held to solar plexus with left hand throughout exercise), at the same time expelling breath carefully to the resonation of "I" as a long EEEEEEEE. Mentally create a condition of timelessness. When the circle is completed, continue the movement by bringing the rod back to first position with right hand while taking a fresh breath, then start circling the rod on the South-North axis while still turning and expelling breath in a resonation of 'A' as in Ahhhhhhhhhhhh, and mentalising spacelessness. When the rod is reaching apex position, take fresh breath, change direction of circle to right angles through West-East axis, resonate the "O" as Ohhhhhhlihhhhhh, and mentalise uneventfulness. Come to rest at original position...

Having established the I.A.O. axes imagine oneself as a globe of pure force within it. Light is a useful medium but it could be radiant energy of any kind proceeding from the exact centre. Unlike light however, it does not get weaker as it gets further from its source, but exerts precisely the same potency at all points of its three fields which is really one field. The energy does nothing, it simply IS. Npw we stat mentally contracting the whole energy field to its centre where we are seeking direct contact with the Supreme Cipher or the Ultimate God. As we contract inwards, calling on the Ultimate by whatever Name we are in the habit of using, we are reducing our everyday selves to Nothing as we feel the circles...closing in around us.

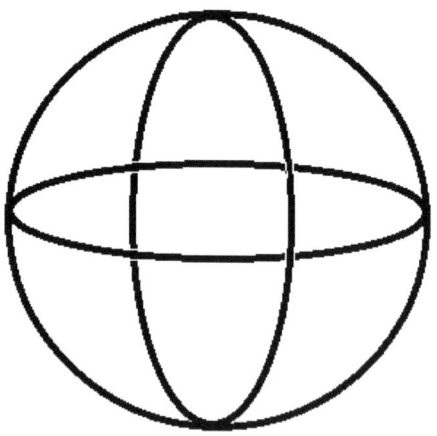

32963498R00147

Printed in Great Britain
by Amazon